Praise for Benjamin Pratt & the Keepers of the School

★"[Readers] will welcome this new demonstration of kid power."
—*Kirkus Reviews* on *We the Children*, starred review

"Clements has the making of an action-lover's dream. . . ."
—*Publishers Weekly* on *We the Children*

"[A] modern kid-power mystery series . . ."
—*Kirkus Reviews* on *Fear Itself*

"Solid writing, likeable characters, danger, a seaside setting, and now treasure will make readers eager for the third installment."
—*School Library Journal* on *Fear Itself*

"Have no fear, because *Fear Itself* is an entertaining and engaging tale about courage, friendship, and respect." —Kidsread.com

WE HOLD
THESE TRUTHS

BENJAMIN PRATT & THE
KEEPERS OF THE SCHOOL

WE HOLD THESE TRUTHS
BOOK 5

ANDREW CLEMENTS

ILLUSTRATED BY ADAM STOWER

Atheneum Atheneum Books for Young Readers
New York London Toronto Sydney New Delhi

atheneum

ATHENEUM BOOKS FOR YOUNG READERS

An imprint of Simon & Schuster Children's Publishing Division

1230 Avenue of the Americas, New York, New York 10020

This book is a work of fiction. Any references to historical events, real people, or real places are used fictitiously. Other names, characters, places, and events are products of the author's imagination, and any resemblance to actual events or places or persons, living or dead, is entirely coincidental.

Text copyright © 2013 by Andrew Clements

Illustrations copyright © 2013 by Adam Stower

All rights reserved, including the right of reproduction in whole or in part in any form.

ATHENEUM BOOKS FOR YOUNG READERS is a registered trademark of Simon & Schuster, Inc.

Atheneum logo is a trademark of Simon & Schuster, Inc.

For information about special discounts for bulk purchases, please contact Simon & Schuster Special Sales at 1-866-506-1949 or business@simonandschuster.com.

The Simon & Schuster Speakers Bureau can bring authors to your live event. For more information or to book an event, contact the Simon & Schuster Speakers Bureau at 1-866-248-3049 or visit our website at www.simonspeakers.com.

Also available in an Atheneum Books for Young Readers hardcover edition

Book design by Sonia Chaghatzbanian

The text for this book is set in ITC Garamond Std.

The illustrations for this book are rendered in pen and ink.

Manufactured in the United States of America

0916 MTN

First Atheneum Books for Young Readers paperback edition November 2014

10 9 8 7 6 5 4 3 2

CIP data for this book is available from the Library of Congress.

ISBN 978-1-4169-3890-3 (hc)

ISBN 978-1-4169-3911-5 (pbk)

ISBN 978-1-4424-9898-3 (eBook)

For Bill and Penny Parke
—A. C.

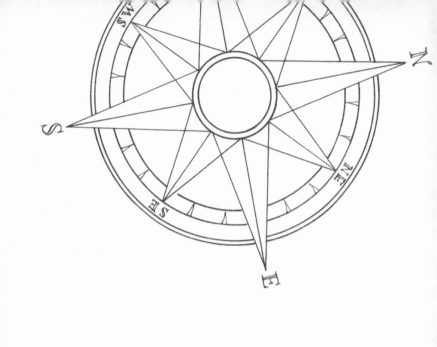

WE HOLD
THESE TRUTHS

CHAPTER 1

Prank

It was seven fifty-five on Monday morning, and Benjamin Pratt was hiding in a huge clump of rhododendron. The bushes were about ten feet away from the path that went toward the Annex, the low building hooked onto the back of the Captain Duncan Oakes School. He was hiding because he knew that Robert Gerritt was going to come walking along here on his way to school in a few minutes, and when he did, Ben was going to jump up and scare the daylights out of him.

It was kind of a stupid idea, but Ben didn't care. This was just for fun . . . and also because Gerritt was usually *way* too serious. A jolt of good old-fashioned panic might loosen the guy up a little.

It hardly seemed like a good moment to be goofing around . . . but that was sort of the point. Yes, the Glennley Group was still planning to demolish the Captain Oakes School this week; and yes, he and Jill and Robert only had two and half days left to stop all that; and yes, once they went inside, the rest of today was going to be risky and stressful and intense. But right now? Time to mess around.

Then something caught Ben's eye, there at the back door of the Annex, the door to the playground.

Is that . . . ? Yes!

It was Wally, lurking in the hallway.

Wally and his boss, Mr. Lyman, worked for the Glennley Group, but they had also been posing as the school janitors, so they were in the building every day.

They didn't know exactly what Ben and Jill and Robert were up to—and they certainly didn't know that the three kids were part of a secret group called the Keepers of the School. And Lyman and Wally also didn't know that the Keepers had a list of clues and that they had already located a bunch of things that the founder of the school had hidden back in the 1700s—things that Captain Oakes had hoped could be used as safeguards to protect his legacy.

But the two fake janitors *did* know that the kids were looking for *something* inside the school *and* that they were dead set against the new theme park that the Glennley company was planning to build here once the school was torn down. So, the two men simply tried to watch them—all day, every day.

Ben had to squint a little to see Wally because of the reflection on the glass of the door, but the guy was definitely there. Well . . . so what? Was that any reason to pass up a perfect chance to prank Gerritt? No way!

Ben was sweating like crazy. This was supposed to turn into a really hot day, and it was already about eighty degrees and very humid. But he tried to ignore the discomfort . . . and also the huge bumblebees that buzzed among the pink and white blossoms.

It was seven fifty-eight now, and he watched as two buses came rumbling into the driveway.

Then glancing back to his left, he spotted Robert. He was coming toward the back of the school along the path from School Street, head down, lost in thought, walking like he was in a huge hurry—same as always.

Ben crouched lower, ready to leap up and scream like a madman.

But before he could move, the door at the back corner of the Annex opened and Wally rushed out. The stocky little man walked quickly across the playground and stopped right in front of Robert, who looked up at him, totally surprised.

Ben wasn't close enough to hear what the man said, but five seconds later he saw Robert's reaction perfectly. Gerritt actually *shoved* Wally! He pushed right past him, and then yelled, "You don't know *anything*!"

Robert steamed ahead past the Annex and went toward the old building, joining the crowd of kids who had gotten off the buses. Wally watched Gerritt a moment, and then, after a shifty look around the school yard, he hurried back to the door he'd come from.

Ben sat still for about half a minute, completely stunned. Then he backed away through the

4

bushes, picked his way out to Washington Street, and ended up standing beside the seawall in front of the school.

The water of Barclay Bay lay flat and calm; hardly a ripple. There was a stream of dark smoke from the funnel of a distant ship, well out to sea. But Ben barely saw it, barely heard the gulls that wheeled above him, their cries sharp in the still morning air.

He felt like he'd just seen something important. Why had Wally wanted to have a secret conversation with Robert?

And what could have made Robert react like that?

Well, I could text Gerritt right now, tell him I saw the whole thing, and ask him what's up . . .

But it might be better to deal with it later, when they could talk face-to-face. Because he'd meet up with Robert during second period language arts, for sure. And if that wasn't the right time, they could talk at lunch.

'Cause I don't want Gerritt to think I was spying on him or something . . .

Besides, maybe Robert would text him during homeroom and tell him all about it.

Yeah, I'd better wait.

CHAPTER 2

On Track

"Can I say something?"

"No, Jill, you *can't*! So just shut up!"

It was the third time Jill had interrupted him, and Robert was getting mad.

So was Mrs. Hinman. With only two more days until the end of the school year, she didn't need one bit of extra commotion in her Monday afternoon social studies class. And the fact that it was almost ninety degrees in her room didn't help.

She glared at Jill. "You'll get your turn in five minutes. Now, *please*, keep quiet!"

Jill didn't back down. "But this isn't what he

agreed to, Mrs. Hinman. All this stuff about the school's history? It's not what's important now. They're tearing the place down on Thursday, and it's going to ruin the whole town! *That's* what we need to be talking about!" She pointed at Robert. "And *he* said we could have a debate about it in class, instead of just giving our dumb little reports. But now Gerritt's trying to get another stupid A-plus!"

Mrs. Hinman stood up. "Jill, that's enough!" She looked at Ben. "You're part of this project—is Jill right? Did the three of you agree to have a debate?"

Ben nodded. "Except, Robert didn't want to. But we voted, and it was two to one. And now Gerritt's not keeping his promise."

"Fine!" shouted Robert, his face almost red. "You want a debate? Bring it on! *I* say that this worn-out old dump of a school needs to go! *I* say it's time for real changes around here, and *I* say that a theme park like Tall Ships Ahoy! will bring some real life back to Edgeport! And I *also* say that a debate is completely dumb, because no matter what anyone says, the new theme park is going to *happen*!"

In two seconds Jill was at the front of the classroom, right in Robert's face, her fists clenched. "Just because it's *going* to happen doesn't mean that it *should* happen, and *that's* what we're debating, blockhead!"

Mrs. Hinman quickly stepped between them.

"*Stop it*—or you can both go cool off in the principal's office! Is that clear?"

They each mumbled something, and Mrs. Hinman went on.

"Now, if this is going to be a proper debate, there have to be rules." Counting them off on her fingers, she said, "Number one: No shouting and no insulting each other. Number two: You have to back up your opinions with facts. And number three: *I* am the timekeeper, and if I say your time is up, you *stop* talking. Agreed?"

Both of them nodded.

Mrs. Hinman turned and said, "Ben, I'm not sure where you fit into this new structure—any ideas?"

He said, "Um . . . ," and shrugged. He looked sort of confused.

But Ben wasn't confused at all, not one bit.

So far, social studies class was right on track—exactly the way he and Jill and Robert had planned it.

CHAPTER 3

Not a Joke

Ben was trying to pay attention to six things at once. And also trying to keep his head from exploding from the heat. A trickle of sweat ran down the side of his cheek, and he wiped it away.

It really *felt* like the last week of school—a June heat wave, ninety degrees and humid, a light breeze from the southwest. Which meant that the cold ocean fifty feet in front of the school was no help at all—unless you actually waded out into the water . . . or went sailing. Ben wanted to sail so badly that he could taste salt water. But it was only more sweat.

He forced himself to focus on the work at hand.

The debate was almost over, and Jill had been great. Robert had been terrific too—a raving jerk, completely over the top, but very persuasive. The whole class had gotten totally involved in both sides of the issue.

As far as Ben could tell, the debate had been pretty much a tie—which was the plan. Jill had argued that the Oakes School should not be torn down, and then explained why a huge theme park on the edge of Barclay Bay was a terrible idea. And Robert had laid out all the reasons why the new amusement park was going to do great things for the town of Edgeport and the whole seacoast area. And both debaters had plenty of chances to challenge each other's facts and opinions.

Now Mrs. Hinman was taking charge again. "All right—and that's all the time we have for the debate. I want to thank both of you. I think we all have a better idea of the issues and ideas now—"

"Yeah," interrupted Robert, "except it still doesn't matter, 'cause the place is getting torn down, like I said."

There was a ripple of laughter in the room

before Mrs. Hinman crushed it with a stony frown. Glaring at Robert, she said, "And the debate is now officially *over* . . . is that clear?"

Ben had to smile. It was pretty brave of Robert to mouth off so much—he was actually risking getting points taken off his grade—something he truly hated.

Before Mrs. Hinman could start anything new, Ben stood up and hurried to the front of the room. He didn't look confused now—more like a kid who had just figured out a job for himself.

"Um, Mrs. Hinman? Would it be okay if I took a quick survey of the class, sort of a public opinion poll? As part of our project?"

"All right . . . but keep it short."

He turned to face the class and then looked down at his clipboard. "So, how many of you are convinced that the new theme park will be good for Edgeport? Could I see a show of hands, please?"

More than half the hands went up, and Ben had to hide his surprise. It was a good thing Robert was just pretending to support the amusement park. . . . The guy knew how to talk. And think.

Ben said, "How many of you feel like the

Oakes School building is too important to just tear it down?" He wrote the number—only ten kids.

"And how many of you strongly agree with most of what Jill had to say?" Only seven kids raised their hands.

"Okay. And one last question: How many of you strongly agree with what most of what Robert had to say?"

He made a few more notes on his paper and then said, "Now, I'd like all of you who strongly agreed with Jill to come to the back of the room for a follow-up discussion—is that okay, Mrs. Hinman?"

She looked at the clock and frowned.

Ben quickly added, "It'll just take a few minutes, I promise."

Mrs. Hinman sighed, but said, "Fine . . . go ahead."

Once Ben and his group were settled in the back corner, Jill fired up the debate again.

"Well," she said to Robert, "I *still* don't see how anybody could think that a huge, noisy amusement park could be good for this town—that's just . . . stupid!"

Robert said, "Yeah? Well, maybe it's *you* that's stupid!"

14

And the argument was off and running again, even louder than before, with lots of kids joining in—mostly on Robert's side.

Ben could see that Mrs. Hinman was doing her best to keep the discussion under control, but she'd pretty much surrendered to Jill and Robert. This class period was shot, and she knew it.

But now Ben tuned all that out.

Sitting on the front edge of a chair, he was still acting like the pollster. But a careful observer might have noticed how nervous he was, might have seen that he gripped the clipboard so tightly that his knuckles were white.

He had seven kids staring at him, three boys and four girls. He'd thought there would have been more. . . . Seven kids wasn't even a third of the class. He took a quick look at the clock—ten minutes left in fifth period.

Ben gulped and tried to smile, looking cautiously into the faces of the kids. "So, here's my first follow-up question: If you learned that there still might be a way that the new theme park could be stopped, would you want to help with that? Show of hands, please."

All seven hands went up right away, and

Ben pretended to write on his clipboard.

"Okay . . . next question: If helping to stop the Oakes School from being torn down meant that you might get into trouble, would you still want to help? And please be completely honest."

Again, all seven hands went up, but a little more slowly.

Now he had to ask the dangerous question, the one that went over the line. From here on, Ben knew he couldn't pretend he was simply conducting a survey.

"So, one last question: If you had to swear an oath on your sacred honor in order to join a secret group that was trying to stop the theme park, would you swear that oath?"

The question could have sounded dumb, could have made kids giggle. But there was nothing funny about the way Ben asked the question, nothing silly in the tone of his voice or the look on his face.

No one even smiled.

A few kids glanced nervously at the others gathered around Ben in a tight semicircle, and then all seven raised their hands.

Instantly, Ben started handing out index cards,

and in a whisper he read what was printed on each one:

On my sacred honor
I swear that I will do all I can
to save the Oakes School from
destruction
And I swear I will keep all that
I do and learn
in complete secrecy

Signed:

He looked each kid directly in the eye. "This is not a joke. I'm asking you to take this oath, right here, right now, and join a secret group called the Keepers of the School. Please—sign your name. Right now."

Time stopped. Ben felt his heart beating, and the air trapped in his lungs felt sharp, almost electric.

Then the kids moved, quickly pulling out pens and pencils, and they wrote their names on the cards.

Ben began to breathe. Still whispering, he said, "Robert and Jill are in on this too!"

He reached into his book bag and started handing out cheap cell phones. "Keep these hidden. The one-digit number marked on the back of your phone? Write that number next to where you signed your name and then give me your card—that way I can know who's got which phone. And if you can, it's really important to stay after school today, even if it's just for fifteen minutes. An hour would be fantastic. And also tomorrow after school, and probably Wednesday, too—even though it's only a half day. So try to figure out a way to do that. You'll get a text about how you can help—each phone is set to vibrate, so keep it close.

"I can't explain more right now, but the most important thing is that you *chose* to help—really, guys, that's *huge*! Sometime tonight, Jill or Robert or I will call and tell you more about what's going on, which is a *lot*. But you all need to know one thing right now: Watch out for Lyman, the tall janitor, and also for Wally, the short one. They both work for the company that's trying to wreck the school. There's stuff we've got to get done inside this building over the next couple of days, and they're trying to stop us. You'll get a text, okay?"

Each kid nodded gravely, the cell phones disappeared, and Ben collected the last few cards. He wished he could have taken a picture of each of their faces. Gabe Dalton looked like he'd just been sworn into the FBI or something, and Jennie Arling's face had gone pale, almost ghostly, except her eyes were incredibly bright. Everyone taking this very seriously—which was good.

Luke Barton leaned forward and whispered, "So . . . does this have anything to do with what you were doing in the hall last week . . . with the baseball? Or is that top secret?"

Ben had to laugh a little. Luke had seen him last Monday, thumping on the posts in the first-floor hallway with a hardball, trying to find a post that sounded like brass instead of wood.

"Yeah," Ben said, "that was *definitely* part of this. But there's no time to explain everything right now. . . . We've got to rejoin the class and act like nothing has happened, okay?"

Gina half raised her hand and whispered, "Um, one more thing, and . . . I know this is going to sound like a stupid question . . . but, like, do I have to keep this a secret from my mom and dad?"

Ben said, "That's not a stupid question at all. Jill and Robert and me? All our parents know what we're doing. And it's not like we're doing stuff that's against the law or anything. But your parents? You'll all have to figure that out on your own. Because some people really want the new theme park to happen, some grown-ups, I mean . . . and kids, too. And if your parents feel that way, then you probably shouldn't tell them. But it's really up to you . . . so I trust you."

Ben looked from face to face again, and smiled. "Like I said, we'll be in touch by phone. You guys are completely *awesome*—thanks!"

As the group got up and started moving toward the front of the classroom, Ben caught Jill looking at him.

She lifted her eyebrows, just a little—a question.

Ben smiled at her and then nodded, just a little. An answer.

CHAPTER 4

That Sinking Feeling

Ben stood with Jill and Robert in the hall outside Mrs. Hinman's room.

"These are the names of the seven new kids, and also the number of the phone I gave each one. I'll put it all in a text to you as soon as I can."

Joey Slade 3
Luke Barton 6
Gabe Dalton 5
Marin Jacoby 1
Jennie Arling 2

Gina Reller 7
Carolynn Eliot 4

Ben watched Jill. As she read over his list, she made a shape with her mouth, the one he hated. It meant something harsh was coming.

She said, "Well . . . all this sounded good last night, but look at this list. I mean, we just recruited a bunch of kids who we barely know, who are completely untested, and who might be totally unreliable."

"Okay, think about it this way," Robert said. "If only *one* of these kids turns out to be useful, then we've grown our in-school forces by thirty-three percent. If two are helpful, then we are sixty-six percent stronger than before, and if three are good, then that's a one hundred percent increase in our numbers. Plus, the Glennley guys don't know about them, so every newbie is *extra* valuable. The possible upside is way better than any possible downside. I mean, even if they all went running to Lyman, or crying to their mommies, it wouldn't matter. They don't actually know *anything*—none of the details. So it's win, win, win—is how I see it."

"Absolutely," Ben said. "Except I'm still not

sure how much help any of them are going to be with what we've got to do after school today, with getting where we need to go. Because we know Lyman and Wally are gonna be on super-high alert."

Before Jill or Robert could reply, the warning bell clanged—two minutes to get all the way to the gym for sixth-period P.E.

Instinctively, all three of them turned and dashed for the staircase.

As he trotted down the steps, Ben tried to answer his own question. He wasn't feeling good about today's objective.

The weekend had been a near disaster—almost game over. Lyman and Wally had broken a water pipe in a third-floor washroom on Saturday afternoon—a trick that had almost scuttled the rest of the school year, which was only three days. If that attack had succeeded, it would have been the end of Oakes School for sure. The place would have been so badly damaged by the flooding that it probably would have been condemned by the town building department. At the very least, that flood would have kept the Keepers from searching for the last two safeguards. As of this moment, they still had a fighting chance, still had access to the building. But these last three days were crucial.

I hope Captain Oakes knew what he was doing!

It wasn't the first time Ben had thought that.

Yes, Captain Oakes had left things hidden around the school, safeguards he hoped would help to preserve the place if someone ever wanted to tear it down and use the oceanfront land for a different purpose. And, yes, the safeguards they'd found were significant: a remarkable addition to the captain's will; a trust fund worth more than eighty million dollars; and then, just last week, some antique Freemasonry gear that had guaranteed them the help of the Grand Master of the Edgeport Masonic lodge—who turned out to be Jill's dad.

Which was weird—*especially* weird, since this had made Jill feel like she had to let her mom in on the secret too. And then Ben had told both *his* parents about the Keepers. So now they had tons of people helping them—but the grown-ups could only help *outside* the school. Inside, it was all up to them—which is why they'd decided to get more kids involved. Based on how hard it had been to discover the first three safeguards, locating two more in just a few days was going to be tough.

Robert had wanted to skip right to the fifth clue, the final safeguard. . . . The three of them had a big argument about that.

And I shut Gerritt down—because the captain was on my side . . . and Jill, too.

Captain Oakes and his original Keepers had left specific instructions about finding each safeguard in order, and not messing with any safeguard that wasn't needed. Plus, on the copper plate where the list of clues was written, there had been a special warning: *Seek the final safeguard* ONLY IF YOU MUST—*for once it is found, our school will change forever.* And the large iron key they'd found in the same place? Almost the same words were scratched into the metal: USE ONLY IF YOU MUST.

As Ben passed the second-floor doorway and kept charging down the stairs, he couldn't shake the feeling that everything was falling apart. Even if they *did* manage to find the last two safeguards, would *anything* stop the Glennley Group? So far, nothing had worked—not even an eighty-eight million-dollar trust fund. And this heat wave? It seemed to make it harder to do everything, including think. The stairwell was like a sauna.

I really *hope Captain Oakes knew what he was doing!*

Because it felt like the school was sinking. The Glennley warship was closing in, starting to turn into the wind, getting ready to fire a dozen cannons all at once, a full broadside.

And what were the Keepers doing? Not much.

Was Jill right about those seven new kids—were they going to be any use at all? This really wasn't the time for bumbling recruits. This was when they needed battle-tested veterans. Now was the time for the heavy guns, for some real power, for—

Ben slammed to a stop, and Jill and Robert plowed into him, almost pinning him to the wall of the first-floor landing.

"Pratt, you idiot!"

That was Gerritt, and before Jill could add anything, Ben said, "Guys, let's cut gym class! Wally's there, or maybe Lyman, waiting for us—we know that. So, we're gonna *skip*!"

Robert looked at Ben like he'd just suggested that they all put on gorilla suits and go rob a bank. "That's *insane*! The teachers'll figure it out, that we cut class!"

"So?" said Ben. "What's more important—the survival of the school, or a little attendance problem?"

Robert was not happy with that answer. But he said, "So . . . like, where would we hide?"

"We're not just gonna hide—we've got more recruiting to do."

Jill glared at him, her face red from the heat and exertion. "No—not until we see if the *other* new ones are any help! We are *not* recruiting more kids!"

Ben grinned as he started back up the stairs. "Who said anything about kids?"

CHAPTER 5

In

"That's quite a story, Benjamin."

"That's only part of it, Mrs. Hinman! There's a lot more, but—"

Mrs. Hinman held up a hand. "So, you're saying that Mr. Lyman works for the company that bought the school? And you three have been fighting some kind of secret war with him for nearly a month?"

"And also the short janitor," Jill said. "Wally works for the Glennley Group too."

Mrs. Hinman was quiet a moment, and Ben saw an idea dawn on her face.

"So . . . the big report you've been working on . . . ?"

Robert said, "That was mostly a way to get more access to the school . . . except we really *do* want those extra-credit points—right, guys?"

Ignoring Gerritt, Ben said, "It sounds crazy, but it's all true, and in a few minutes we can show you everything we've got, all the proof. But first you're going to have to help us out a little, like really soon."

Mrs. Hinman shook her head and took out a pad of bright yellow hall passes.

"The only help I can offer is permission to get to your sixth-period class. I really can't—"

"But don't you want to keep the school the way it's supposed to be?" Jill asked. "I thought you cared about *real* history and about this town!"

Mrs. Hinman flashed her a sharp look. "Don't think that I'm happy about this, young lady! Two years ago my husband and I bought a house seven blocks from here. I *love* this school, and now, instead of me being able to walk to work, we're going to have to get a second car. Plus, the value of our home has fallen into the ocean. So don't give me a lecture about caring!" She paused, and her cheeks turned bright pink. "I'm . . . I'm sorry . . . but I just don't think there's much I could do, even if everything you've told me is true."

Ben said, "Well, you're about to get some proof about *that*. Shh . . . listen!"

Everyone went still, and they heard heavy footsteps echoing in the stairwell across from the classroom door.

Ben looked Mrs. Hinman in the eye and whispered, "Would it seem like a strange coincidence if one of the so-called janitors wanted to come and look around your room *right now*?" Then, to Jill and Robert, he said, "Quick, into that closet!"

In seconds the three of them were crammed into the coat closet at the back of the room. Jill grabbed the hook on the inside of the door and pulled it shut.

Ben was stuffed into the middle, and he tried to stay completely still. He also tried to stop sweating. Which was impossible. But he had to breathe, and he could smell Jill's hair—some kind of fruity shampoo . . . maybe strawberry. And then he got a good whiff of Gerritt's armpit, which spoiled the moment. He almost whispered, *Dude, you need some* serious *deodorant!* But he didn't want to risk an explosion of giggles.

There was a quiet knock at the classroom door.

"Come in," called Mrs. Hinman. "Oh—hi, Jerry."

"Sorry to bother you, but I wanted to be sure there wasn't any electrical damage from the weekend flood. Mind if I check a couple wall outlets?"

"No, not at all."

Ben heard a muffled clank—Lyman's canvas tool bag. Then there were some rustling sounds, a few clicks, and then a loud electronic beep.

Lyman grunted a little, and then there was another beep.

"Looks like things are okay. Any problems with the overhead lights?"

"No, everything's been fine. So . . . are you checking all the classrooms?"

"Trying to—been putting in a lot of extra hours these past few days. Well," Lyman said, "glad everything's all right."

"Me too—thanks, Jerry."

There were footsteps, and then Ben heard the classroom door close.

Jill whispered, "I can't breathe. . . . Can we get out now?"

Ben felt her start to push the door.

"Stop!" he hissed.

Lyman's voice: "Sorry—forgot my meter."

"No problem."

Footsteps in, footsteps out, and the door closed again.

Ben whispered, "Count to thirty."

After twenty seconds or so, Mrs. Hinman called softly, "He's gone."

Ben followed Jill into the brightness, and blinking, he saw the teacher standing next to the closed classroom door, peering out sideways down the hall.

She glanced at the three of them, and raising one eyebrow, she said, "He didn't go to any other rooms. Sit there in the back, away from the doorway."

Mrs. Hinman pulled up a chair and said, "All right. Tell me everything. And then tell me what you need me to do. As long as I don't have to break any laws, I'm *in*!"

CHAPTER 6

The Whole Crew

Ben looked from face to face to face. "So, we're clear about what each of us has to do?"

Jill and Mrs. Hinman nodded, and Gerritt said, "Clear as a bell."

Hiding out in room thirty-four during sixth period, they'd come up with a new plan, a different way to launch Monday's after-school operation. And Mrs. Hinman had offered some good ideas—in fact, she now had a key role to play.

They had told her everything, start to finish, and Robert had also given her one of the new ghost cell phones—number eight. She was completely plugged in to the Keepers network.

But as the final bell of the school day got closer, Ben felt new doubts crawling into his skull.

Yes, pulling Mrs. Hinman into the Keepers had been his idea . . . but now he wasn't sure how he felt about it.

Now I've got to deal with another grown-up!

Ben was startled by that half-angry thought.

So . . . what am I saying? Am I worried that with more grown-ups on board, I'm not gonna be such a big cheese anymore? And if the Keepers actually get some results, that maybe other people will end up getting all the credit?

He almost blushed, sitting there between Jill and Robert.

Am I really that selfish? And shallow? And . . . ambitious?

Ben knew about wars. He also knew about big battles, the kind that change the course of history—like the Battle of Hastings, and the Battle of Waterloo; like Yorktown, and, of course, Gettysburg. He knew that it was the commanding officers who got the glory—or the blame. And he knew that *his* leadership role in the Keepers seemed to be slipping away . . . or at least getting watered down. A *lot*.

And Ben was keenly aware that what had been happening in and around the Oakes School for the past month, *this* was the Battle of Edgeport. This battle was a crucial episode in the long history of the town—a town that had looked out over the Atlantic Ocean for more than three hundred years. The actions of the next few days were going to have a huge impact on the town and the whole region for generations to come.

So . . . what do I really want out of all this?

Change could not be stopped. Ben was sure of that.

Just two months ago, his own mom and dad had announced that they needed to be separated for a while, that they had some things to work out. Since then, Ben had lived one week with his mom at their house on Walnut Street, and the next week with his dad on their old sailboat at Parson's Marina. He understood just how quickly everything could get turned upside down.

So . . . what do I really want?

Ben knew the answer to that.

He wanted things to be like they used to be.

He wanted his family back, the *whole* family—Mom, Dad, their dog Nelson, and him—everybody on the same crew, everybody under the same roof again, every night. And he wanted the school to stay the same too. It felt like losing the school would be one change too many, a huge chunk of his life—of the whole town's life—gone forever.

Still, there was no use pretending things were always going to stay the same. That wasn't going to happen.

Change couldn't be stopped . . . but people always had choices, didn't they? Even if change was being forced on you—by parents, or by a team of smart lawyers and industrial spies—you still had a choice: You could either give up and accept someone else's ideas about change, or you could fight for the kind of changes you believed in.

So . . . I guess the Keepers are changing too—because we have to.

Parents and grandparents were involved, brand-new kids were involved—and maybe some of them really *would* tell their parents . . . and *that* thought made something snap clear: Today, after social studies, when Gerritt had said that thing about the new Keepers telling "their mommies"?

That was a wisecrack, a put-down of him and Jill—because they had both told their parents everything.

On Sunday afternoon, Jill had been pretty tough on Gerritt, telling him he needed to stop being so touchy about family stuff—which he kind of had the right to be. After all, his mom and dad had died in a car crash when he was five years old . . . something Ben couldn't imagine. And Robert had seemed to lighten up a little. But that was yesterday. Today, it was pretty much the same old Gerritt, sharp and sarcastic.

Or . . . was today's shift mostly because of that run-in he'd had with Wally before school?

Ben still hadn't had a chance to talk to Robert about that. It felt like Gerritt had been avoiding him all morning, and at lunch he'd barely said two words—and one of them had been, "Duh!"

No way around it: Gerritt was being a real blockhead today.

But he didn't care what Robert thought, or what kind of wisecracks the guy made about "mommies." Ben was glad he'd told his parents—because now they were actually talking to each other again.

Because they both want to help me.

And it was also clear that Jill had done the right thing when she'd gotten her mom involved. In fact, without Mrs. Acton, they wouldn't have discovered the starting point for this afternoon's search. Because on Saturday morning, Jill had shown her mom the full set of safeguard clues:

After five bells sound, time to sit down.
After four times four, tread up one more.
After three books pass, one will be brass.
After two tides spin, a man walks in.
After one still star, horizons afar.

Then Jill had explained exactly how they had solved the first three clues—which was important, because each solution revealed more about the way Captain Oakes was thinking as he planned. And Mrs. Acton really got it. She understood how every word of each clue had a meaning— concealed, but mostly hidden in plain sight.

And looking at the next clue they had to solve, "after two tides spin," she'd had an idea right away: "I'll bet that has something to do with a tide mill!"

She'd explained to Jill that since Colonial times

in America, there had been about three hundred tide mills along the Atlantic coast.

The idea behind a tide mill was simple. In Barclay Bay, for example, the difference between high tide and low tide was about ten feet, and there were two high tides and two low tides each day. To make a tide mill, workers had to dig a channel for water to rush into during the high tide, and they also had to dig a pool or a pond for that water to fill. After the rising tide filled the pool, the channel was closed to trap the water—at a level ten feet higher than the low tide. Then about six hours later at low tide, the channel was unblocked to let water flow down out of the pool to rejoin the ocean. That falling water was directed to a water wheel, and the power from that spinning wheel could be used to run a loom to weave cloth, or spin a blade to saw wood, or turn millstones to grind flour.

Because of the mess with the flood at the school, Jill hadn't texted the tide mill idea to anyone until late Sunday afternoon, and after she did, Tom Benton immediately texted everyone back.

Another grown-up . . .

Tom had been the janitor at the Oakes School

a long time ago—he'd had the job before Mr. Keane. And it was Roger Keane who had recruited Ben to lead the Keepers . . . and then had died the very same day.

Also a grown-up . . .

Tom's text said he recalled Mr. Keane once telling him about a wooden water wheel down in the basement of the school.

Right away, Ben had called Tom to ask for more particulars, but the man didn't have much more to add—except for one very important detail:

"Did I say the mill wheel was in the basement? Because I *meant* to say that it was in the *sub*-basement."

"The school has *two* basements?" Ben asked. "Because the building plans we studied in the library only showed one."

"Not many folks know about the lower level."

"How do you get to it?"

Tom had answered slowly. "Well . . . I don't really know. I never went down there, never needed to. Seems to me that Roger said the entrance was somewhere near the big boilers . . . or maybe it was along the east wall. . . . I guess you'll have to hunt around a bit."

That conversation with Tom had happened around six p.m., and it wasn't until after nine on Sunday night that he and Jill and Robert had worked out the plan for recruiting more kids to help inside the school.

As all this ran through his mind, Ben suddenly saw something with perfect clarity, and it seemed so obvious that he felt totally stupid—for about the hundredth time. On a gold coin, Captain Oakes had written, MY SCHOOL WILL ALWAYS BELONG TO THE CHILDREN, but who did he entrust the coin to? A grown-up, the first janitor. And then, on the copper plate he and Jill had found hidden behind the floor molding, it had said, WE THE CHILDREN WILL ALWAYS BE THE KEEPERS OF THE SCHOOL—and that statement had been signed by three kids. But it wasn't children who had built the school, or hidden the safeguards, or paid the taxes to keep the school working for the past two centuries—all that had been done by grown-ups!

But . . . how come the captain got those three kids involved at the start, back in 1791? Or . . . was it even the captain who had made that decision? Maybe John Vining, the carpenter, had been the one who decided to recruit his son and two other kids. . . .

Thinking about all of it made Ben's head spin— or was that just the heat again? Anyway, if he and Jill and Robert plus all the rest of the crew could keep the school from being demolished, there would be plenty of time to do more research and try to answer all the questions. Because history was never simple.

The bell clanged—sixth period was over.

It was time to stop thinking about history. It was time to go and make some. Because if Mrs. Hinman, the newest grown-up Keeper, could execute her part of today's plan, he and Jill and Robert were about to launch a pretty bold mission.

To find this hidden tide mill, they had to get into the *sub*-basement—but first they would have to get down to the basement. And to get into the basement they were going to have to walk right through the middle of enemy headquarters—the janitor's workroom.

CHAPTER 7

Outlet

Three minutes after the final bell, Robert sent a text to the cell phones of all seven of the new kids: Can you tell me where Lyman or Wally is? It was the first test of their communication system—the disposable cell phones Tom Benton had bought at Target on Sunday night.

Almost instantly, five of the new recruits replied. Two said, No. But the other three had good information: Marin and Gina reported that Lyman was on the first floor, standing near the south stairwell, and Gabe had spotted Wally, also on the ground floor, sweeping the floors near the north stairwell.

Ben smiled. The Glennley goons were on the lookout for the three kids who had skipped gym class. Lyman and Wally had started using walkie-talkies to coordinate, and they had placed themselves so they could observe all four  of the first-floor hallways of the old building.

Thinking like a general now, Ben said, "We've got to get Lyman to move out of position so we can get to the janitor's room."

Mrs. Hinman smiled and said, "I'll have him right here inside this room in five minutes or less, guaranteed!"

She walked over and clicked the intercom button on the wall by her door.

"Yes? May I help you?" It was Mrs. Hendon, the school secretary. The old speaker below the clock made her voice sound fuzzy.

Mrs. Hinman replied, "Hi, Rita, I know this is a terrible time of day for you, but I need some help.

Could you send Jerry up here? He checked out the electrical circuits in my classroom this afternoon, and now the outlet I need to run my digital projector is dead. I've got to have it working first period tomorrow—or maybe he could just bring me a heavy extension cord. But I'm worried about the outlet. I keep thinking that I hear some sort of noise, like maybe some kind of crackling or something. I think he'd better come right away, if you can reach him."

"Sounds serious, June—I'll get him up there as soon as possible!"

"Thanks, and could you buzz me back when he's on his way?"

"Sure will!"

And Mrs. Hendon was gone.

"That's great!" Jill said. "And that stuff about the noise was genius!"

Robert frowned. "Well, *I* think it was pretty stu—"

Ben saw Gerritt suddenly remember that he was talking to a teacher.

He blushed a little, then said, "What I *meant* to say is, it might have been a good idea to explain a little before you started saying all that, Mrs.

Hinman. Because Lyman just tested the outlets, and they *work*, and when he finds out that they *still* work, it's going to make him suspicious . . . is the only problem I see."

Mrs. Hinman didn't seem to hear him. She was on the move, shoving desks this way and that, clearing an area near the center of the room.

She pointed. "Jill and Robert, would you grab that small table and bring it here? Just set the globe on the floor in the corner. And, Ben, get the projector from the cabinet back there to the left of the coat closet."

After the table was placed, she said, "Robert, pull down that screen behind my desk. . . . Good."

Robert wasn't used to being ignored. "Um . . . Mrs. Hinman? About the outlet . . ."

Ben said, "I don't see the projector back here."

"Did I say the left cabinet? I meant the *right* one—I'm always doing that!"

Ben found it and carried it to the table.

Robert said, "Mrs. Hinman, I really think the outlet thing could be a problem. Maybe we should . . ."

The intercom speaker crackled, followed by a soft clang—a recording of the ship's bell that hung in the school office.

Mrs. Hendon said, "June? Jerry's on his way, should be there in just a few minutes."

"Great, Rita. Thanks a lot!"

The speaker clicked off, and Mrs. Hinman motioned to Robert.

"Here, take a look." She pointed just below the projector table, and Ben saw a square brass plate on the floor, set just below the surface of the wood. In the center of the plate there was a single round electrical outlet.

She looked at Robert and winked. "*That's* the outlet Mr. Lyman is going to try to fix—and it hasn't worked for about seven years. Now, you three better get out of here. I'll text you when our helpful janitor is good and busy!"

CHAPTER 8

Running the Blockade

When he stepped out of room thirty-four with Jill and Robert, Ben felt like he was sailing into enemy waters. Lyman and Wally had been working hard to establish control of the whole building, and they were getting good at it.

The plan for the next five minutes was simple: The three of them were going to hang out in the west hallway opposite from Mrs. Hinman's room and wait until Lyman was busy. Then they'd sneak down the south stairs to the first-floor hallway, turn left, walk about fifty feet, and take another left into the janitor's room. Then it was a straight shot down into the basement.

Ben's phone buzzed—a text on his ghost phone. He looked at it, and said, "It's Gina—Lyman just came out of the janitor's room, and he's headed for the south stairwell!"

Jill grabbed her phone too. "This is from Gabe—Wally's coming upstairs too, north stairwell!"

Ben looked around. He'd thought that Wally would stay at his sentry post on the first floor—they had to hide!

"Quick," Robert said, "this way!" And he dashed for the stairwell—the south one.

"No!" Jill gasped. "Lyman's coming *up*!"

Robert kept moving. "Yes, up to the *third* floor. So we need to get down and then out onto the *second* floor before he sees us, *NOW*!"

Kids were still hurrying down the south stairwell toward the buses, and there was plenty of yelling and talking. The noise of three more kids running downstairs didn't stand out, but that didn't make Ben feel any less scared. If Lyman spotted them, this day would be a total loss.

Following Robert and Jill, he made it to the second-floor landing, then to the door.

"Hey!" Lyman yelled.

Ben jumped and then stopped, his fingers still on the crash-bar.

"Slow down there, young fella!"

Lyman was below, yelling at someone else.

Ben scrambled through the doorway, and Jill grabbed his arm and pulled him around the corner to the right.

"This way," she whispered, "in case Wally comes onto this floor—I've got Gabe tailing him!"

They sped away, and Ben thought he heard Lyman's heavy footsteps . . . but the second-floor door didn't open, and he began breathing again.

He put on a burst of speed and reached the southwest corner of the hallway in seconds.

"Mr. Pratt—*stop* right there, please."

It was a man's voice, but Ben didn't look to see who it was. He didn't have to. There was only one teacher who called him Mr. Pratt.

He turned and smiled. Sweat trickled down his forehead and he wiped it away, trying to look unflustered. And obviously failing.

"Oh—hi, Mr. Collins."

The science teacher stood in his doorway. The

afternoon sunshine framed him, making his white shirt look almost orange.

"Ah-ha—and I see we have Miss Acton and Mr. Gerritt here as well: three students running in *my* hallway." He paused, scrunching up his mouth. "A hypothesis: You're late for buses. . . . No, wrong direction for that. Or perhaps playing tag . . . No, much too warm. Could this be an attack of sheer, uncontrollable, last-week-of-school insanity? Yes, that's the one I'll go with. . . . Am I correct?"

Ben hesitated, and Gerritt stepped in—which still happened a little too often.

"Almost, sir—we just got a little too enthusiastic! We're working on an extra-credit assignment for social studies."

Mr. Collins frowned and narrowed his eyes at Robert. "And you have empirical evidence to support this wild assertion?"

Ben smiled. It was two smart guys, trying to out-geek each other. Funny, except they didn't have time for this.

But Gerritt was just getting warmed up. He grinned as he spoke. "Yes, indeed. We have visually tangible and measurable evidence, Mr. Collins: three chemically tinted polygons of compressed organic matter issued by competent authorities, complete with manually applied symbols composed of graphite and assorted polymer compounds. Here . . ."

It took Ben a second to figure out that Gerritt was talking about their yellow hall passes—the ones Mrs. Hinman and the school librarian had signed. He and Jill followed Robert's lead and held out their slips for inspection.

From the corner of his eye, Ben saw Jill glance down at her phone.

The teacher cleared his throat to reply to Robert, but Jill spoke first, softly, as if she was sharing a secret.

"Um, Mr. Collins, could we all step into your room a second? Like right now? We've got to ask you a few questions, important questions. About our project. Right *now*."

Ben didn't get it until Jill actually pushed him straight toward Mr. Collins, who had no choice but to back up into his room. Jill had to be reacting to news about Wally—he must be getting closer!

Jill grabbed Robert and pushed him into the room too, then pulled the door shut.

Out in the hall Ben heard the footsteps coming, heavier and slower than Lyman's, also more rapid—Wally was at least a foot shorter.

Jill heard the footsteps too.

She steered everyone toward the back of the room, toward a place where Wally couldn't see them unless he actually stepped inside. She talked softly as she moved them away from the door. "Back there . . . um, on that lab table? Have you ever noticed . . . the valves for the Bunsen burners? They're . . . made of brass, and, look . . . they're

stamped with a name . . . no, it's a city—Columbus, Ohio. Do you have any idea when these were installed—in the history of the school?"

For just a second, Mr. Collins looked at Jill as if she needed a brain transplant. But she kept her face completely serious, completely sincere. So, the science teacher tried to answer her question.

"Yes . . . well, um . . . judging from the metal work—because that's a brass casting and not a stamped fixture—I'd estimated that this piping was installed sometime just after 1900. I know for a fact that Robert Bunsen's design for a laboratory heat source was in wide use by the 1860s or so, but a school like this one wouldn't have installed them until much later. And now, of course, the gas is all disconnected, because we don't need burners for the middle-grade science curriculum. That kind of compounding and combinatory experimentation doesn't begin in most public school districts until the eighth grade. Does . . . does that answer your question?"

Ben knew the answer to that—Wally's footsteps had passed the room, so the danger was past.

Jill nodded. "Yes, that's great, Mr. Collins. I've

always wondered about that—about that part of the history of the school."

"Hmm . . . that's interesting," he said.

And again Ben saw that same puzzled look on the guy's face.

"Well, thanks," said Jill. "We've got to go now—a lot more research for our project. And we won't run in the halls any more, right, guys?"

"Absolutely," Ben said. "No more running."

The second they were alone in the hallway again, Ben texted their spy network: Any sign of Wally?

Gabe replied, and Ben relayed the info.

"Wally's in the library now—let's move!"

Back to the south stairwell, down to the first floor, then a quick fifty paces to the left. The janitor's room door was open, but there was hallway traffic, kids and teachers.

Ben went to the drinking fountain across the hall, and Jill and Robert got in line behind him. When the coast was clear, they all slipped into the workroom.

Ben walked straight to the red door, just to the right of the long workbench. It was unlocked.

In fact, there was a sign above the knob that read FIRE DOOR—DO NOT LOCK. The other sign on the door was framed with yellow-and-black stripes. CAUTION: STEPS DOWN.

Ben whispered, "Get out your headlamps—ready?"

He pulled the door open, and Jill and Robert followed him into the darkness.

CHAPTER 9

This Way Down

At least it's cooler down here!

In the dim light at the bottom of the steps Ben could see the huge granite blocks that formed the outer foundation of the building. Everywhere else, it was dark. They had come down nine steps to the basement floor, and the glow filtering from the small window in the door didn't reach very far into the blackness.

Ben clicked his LED headlamp on to low power, and it threw out a narrow shaft of white light. As he looked around, the beam jumped from one unfamiliar object to another. Jill and Robert also turned their lights on, and the beams began poking about randomly. He felt like the area was mostly open, but he wasn't able to get much sense of the whole space.

"Hey, guys," he called in a loud whisper, "let's stay together and try to map things out a little. We've got to get our bearings. Hey—listen!"

The school's bell was ringing above them—four clangs, which meant the last bus was leaving. It reminded Ben of a channel bell buoy on a foggy day, muffled and distant. He heard footsteps above them too, on the hallway floor. But again, the sounds seemed faint and far away.

In the quietness, they all heard something else, off in the darkness—little rustlings and scurryings.

"Rats!" squeaked Jill. "Why do we always have to hang out with the rats!"

Ben had to smile. It took a lot to get Jill flustered, and he sort of enjoyed it.

He said, "The ancestors of those rats might have sailed here from England with Captain Oakes's ancestors. They've got just as much right to be here as we do."

Robert said, "How fascinating. And don't forget that rat rhymes with Pratt."

Another wisecrack, but Ben ignored Gerritt and pulled out a pencil and the clipboard he'd used during social studies. "We know the janitor's room is on the south side of the school, so if I stand here with the doorway on my right, it means I'm facing east—toward the ocean."

On a blank piece of paper he drew a large rectangle, and then marked a directional letter on each side—*E, N, W, S*.

"Okay," he said, "so let's walk to the east wall and work our way around to the left from there. Tom said he thought the entrance to the sub-basement was near the boilers—but I don't really know what we're looking for."

Ben stood still, drawing evenly spaced little squares to indicate the placement of the massive wooden posts that supported the building above them.

"C'mon, move it, Pratt," said Robert. "You don't have to create a masterpiece."

"Yeah, I know," Ben said, but he stayed hunched over his clipboard.

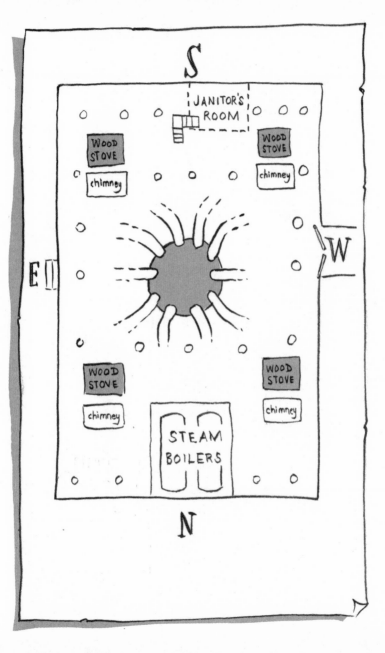

"Here's a chimney," Jill said. "A big one. And some kind of iron furnace."

Ben guessed that the brick chimney was about twenty feet from the southeast corner of the basement. It measured at least four feet on each side, and the brickwork rested on four large granite blocks. Bending over to shine his light directly at the floor, he was surprised to see the surface wasn't concrete—more like a mix of sand and dirt and crushed seashells, packed tight and flat.

Robert said, "I think I'd call that thing a stove instead of a furnace—looks like it burned wood. Yeah . . . see? White ashes—definitely a jumbo-size woodstove."

Ben was adding the chimney and woodstove to his drawing when Robert gave a low whistle, and said, "What is *that*?"

Ben followed the beam of Robert's headlamp. A large round tube hung from the low ceiling, and it ran twenty or thirty feet to an enormous domed structure. More big tubes, at least ten of them, seemed to sprout from the top of the dome.

"We had one just like that in the basement at our house," said Ben, "except about ten times smaller. Same thing, though. My dad called it

an octopus furnace. This stuff we're seeing? It's all from different time periods—the woodstove probably came right after they stopped using the upstairs fireplaces. Then they burned coal under that big octopus dome. And look," he added, aiming his headlight upward at the black metal pipes hanging from the ceiling beams, "those pipes come from the boiler, the newest heater. And the boiler sends hot water to all the radiators in the school."

Pretending to yawn, Gerritt said, "Thank you, Professor Pratt. You can draw all the little maps you want, but this place gives me the creeps, and the sooner I'm out, the better! I don't know about you guys, but *I'm* following those water pipes straight to where Tom said we should look for the entrance to the sub-basement—which *is* why we're here, right?"

Ben wanted to keep exploring. He saw that there were actually four of the old iron woodstoves, each with its own chimney. But he tucked the drawing into his backpack and followed Robert toward the boilers.

Jill called softly from the north corner. "Hey—I found an opening!"

Ben hurried over and saw a boarded-up gap in the foundation, about four feet wide and three feet high.

Gerritt came too, and right away he said, "False alarm—see at the bottom there, the way those boards are slanted? I think that used to be a chute for dumping firewood or coal down here. And the boards here on the floor? Probably to keep the fuel from getting damp."

Ben looked down. On either side of the chute's opening, the floor was covered with wide oak planks that made a rectangle about fifteen feet wide and ten feet out from the wall.

Jill turned and started to walk toward the west wall, then suddenly stopped.

"Hey, something moved!" she whispered.

Gerritt grinned. "Probably just a big rat."

"No," she said, "I felt the *floor* move—under my feet. And listen . . . hear that?" She tapped her foot, first on one plank, then on its neighbor. The second plank had a hollow sound.

"Look!" Robert said. "A handle!"

Ben used his phone to snap a quick photo of the place Gerritt was pointing, and the flash practically blinded them. But they all saw a flat iron ring about four inches across, set into the thick oak floorboard so that it lay flush with the surface. It was caked with dirt and coal dust, almost invisible. Six inches in front of the ring, three of the wide boards were cut in a straight line. Ben walked along the center plank, the one with the handle, and about eight feet away, there was another straight cut across the same three boards.

Ben felt the boards move—Robert had already pried the handle loose, and using both hands, he was pulling upward.

Ben jumped to one side, and with a quiet groan from the hinges, Robert's end of the hatch's cover rose up until it was higher than his head. When he let go, the door stayed open, like one of those long lids on the bed of a pickup truck.

"Cool!" said Robert. "There's a weight-and-pulley system—I could have lifted that thing with one hand!" Waving his arm like a cheesy magician, he smiled and said, "Ladies and gentlemen, this way down!"

CHAPTER 10

Below
Below

A breath of even cooler air came flowing up into Ben's face as he followed Robert and Jill down into the sub-basement. Blocks of gray granite had been stacked to make simple steps, twelve of them. Straight ahead at the bottom there was a small space—just enough room for the chains and pulleys that kept the door raised. He did a double take when he saw the weights—two large rusty cannonballs hung at the end of each chain. Ben tilted his head back and looked up at the hatch suspended above him. The bottom of the

Hatchway to below below

E

cannon
balls

FOUNDATION
WALL

cut through
foundation wall

← sub basement →
space

three wide oak planks had been sheathed with copper—the whole thing had to weigh several hundred pounds.

Robert said, "Better pull down that cover, don't you think?"

Jill shook her head, and the beam of her headlamp whipped back and forth across Robert's face. "No way!"

Robert shrugged. "Okay, but don't blame me if Wally or Lyman comes and finds us."

"I don't care if the whole Glennley army shows up—that thing stays *open!*"

Ben said, "I agree with Jill. . . . I mean, who knows? We might need to get out in a hurry."

That was not what she'd wanted to hear, and for a second Jill looked like she was going to bolt right back up the steps. But she turned around and followed Robert into the darkness.

Getting his bearings again, Ben realized that this wasn't really the school's sub-basement. Yes, the floor was lower than the level of the school basement, but looking to his right at the bottom of the stairs, an opening about three feet wide had been cut through the foundation of the north wall of the school. And beyond that, there was a completely different space, a cavern that had been dug into the earth below the north lawn—not underneath the school building at all.

As Ben stepped through the cut in the foundation wall, he could actually *feel* the space opening out in front of him—and he also imagined that he felt the weight of the earth above him. A quick burst of panic hit him, and he pictured the roof giving way, imagined those deadly tons of dirt and rock and trees crushing the air out of his lungs. And there'd be no way to call for help—no cell phone signal this far underground.

But swiveling his head around, the light quickly showed him that Captain Oakes and John Vining had not taken any chances. Every ten feet or so, a stack of sturdy granite blocks rose from floor to ceiling, and the floor down here was granite, wide paving slabs, most of them two or three feet square. The ceiling was high, at least ten feet, and it was solid, too—thick oak planks crisscrossing, and every place where the earth touched a plank, the wood had been covered with that same copper sheathing he'd noticed on the hatchway door. Ben smiled, and he remembered the name of the book they had found in the school library almost four

weeks ago: *A Man of the Sea, A School for the Ages.*
Everything the captain left behind had been built
to endure.

All noise from the school had disappeared,
but it wasn't quiet. Ben heard the sound of water
dripping and gurgling all around him. And there
was no mistaking the smell: It was salt water.

There was another distinct odor that was harder
for Ben to identify. He followed his nose, and his
headlamp cleared up the mystery instantly—rotting
wood, lots of it.

Ben snapped picture after picture. He wanted
to document everything, wanted to be able to
study the images later, back at his dad's boat.
Because centuries ago, workmen had built a system
of elevated troughs and chutes down here, wooden
channels to move the seawater around in this man-
made cavern. Which made sense: If there really
was a tide mill down here, the main ingredient
was water.

The wooden support posts and the close-fitted
planks were mostly rotted and fallen, but he could
still get a sense of how they must have looked.
They reminded him of the wooden structures
he'd seen in photos of old mining camps in the

Klondike, where streams had been diverted into wooden culverts to help the men wash away the gravel to find gold.

"Hey," Jill called softly, "check it out—lanterns!"

Ben saw them too. About half of the granite foundation stacks had iron hooks driven between the blocks about six feet above the floor, and from each hook hung a square tin lamp. Through the sooty glass in the one closest to him, he saw the stub of a candle.

Walking directly to the east wall, Ben wasn't surprised to see more granite blocks. Water trickled down the rock and pooled in a trough cut into the floor beside the wall. And he could see that the trough was slanted so the water would flow to the left, which was north.

He turned around and walked straight back to the west wall. It was also made of granite blocks . . . except these were much larger, some of them as wide as four feet, and all were at least two feet thick. Moving closer with his headlamp, Ben saw that the top, bottom, and sides of each huge block had been carefully smoothed—the cracks between them were hardly thicker than a piece of paper.

And Ben suddenly understood why: The wooden chutes had carried the water into a reservoir behind this wall, and this was the dam, holding back the water so it could be released to run the tide mill—genius!

Grabbing his clipboard, he started to sketch how the water must have flowed, but a soft call from Robert stopped him.

"Hey, guys, I found the water wheel!"

Ben trotted over to the northwest corner of the space. Gerritt stood beside a wooden structure, kind of a shed. On the other side of the shed, almost touching the north foundation wall, he saw a rounded arc made of wood. He walked along the walls of the shed to his right until he could see around the far corner of the little building, and there it was—definitely a mill wheel.

He took a photo and then snapped more pictures as he walked eastward along the north wall. He was following the mill race, a channel about two feet wide and at least that deep, down below the floor level. The channel ended at the east wall, and he took a picture of the outlet, the place where the water would have flowed back into the ocean at low tide. The hole had been plugged with a big square granite block, sealed in place with something that looked like tar.

From back at the shed, Jill called out, "Robert, don't go any farther—that floor's rotten!"

"Hey, chill," he said. "It's not like I'm gonna drop into a mineshaft or something—the ground is only two feet down."

"Well, you could still get hurt."

Ben was beside her now, looking in at the doorway of the shed, and he agreed—the floor looked bad.

"See where the plank ends are nailed?" he said to Robert. "That's where the floor joists are—they should be pretty solid."

Robert wasn't listening.

"After two tides spin, a man walks in. . . . After two tides spin, a man walks in. . . ."

Robert was muttering the clue over and over as he shined the light from his headlamp every which way inside the small structure.

Ben wanted to look more closely and also take pictures. He stepped up into the shed and felt the whole structure shift a little—not a good sign. But he got his footing on a solid spot, and took a good photo of the two millstones in the center of the shed. They weren't big—less than two feet across. The wooden shafts and gears that had turned them had begun to rot, and a lot of the support structure had slipped to one side and collapsed into a jumble that looked like giant nursery blocks.

The more he looked around, the less sense it made to him. Why go to all this trouble to build such a tiny mill? And why hide it away like this?

He took a closer look at the millstones—they were totally black . . . and the floor all around the stones looked the same way, a deep, ground-in sooty color.

Ben reached down, rubbed the blackened floorboard, and then sniffed the smudge on his fingers . . . and the smell called up an image: the smoke from the cannons that were fired in front of town hall on the Fourth of July.

"That's it!" he exclaimed. "That's what Captain Oakes was doing down here—he was grinding

gunpowder! And he didn't want King George to know about it!"

"Gunpowder?" said Jill. "You mean he could just *make* it? Right here? That is so cool!"

It was like Robert hadn't even heard what Ben said.

"After two tides spin, a man walks in. . . . After two tides . . . Okay, so, like, I get the part about the spinning, right? That's the wheel, and it spins after a high tide and a low tide—two tides. But 'a man walks in'? A man walks in . . . *what*? Or, in *where*? That's what we don't know."

Jill was still standing outside the shed.

"Well," she said, "when you walk *in*, that means you're going *into* something—some kind of a room or an enclosed space. And to get into a room, there's usually a door. So, maybe it's that one."

And she pointed at a simple door on the wall to the left of the millstones, just four vertical boards with a couple of cross pieces, hanging on two rusty hinges. It was fastened shut with a bent nail.

Robert rolled his eyes. "Duh, Jill. That was the first place I looked."

"Mind if I look too?" asked Ben.

"Knock yourself out, professor."

Robert turned the nail and pulled the door open, and Ben looked through the opening with him, still being careful about where he stepped. They had a clear view of the inside structure that braced the water wheel.

"Hmm, what a surprise," said Robert sarcastically, shining his light this way and that. "Dead end, same as the *first* time I looked. Any other bright ideas, Jill?"

Ben didn't see anything unusual. "I guess this was just how they got at the inside of the wheel, to work on the spokes and the hub and stuff." He didn't want Jill to think he was making fun of her idea the way Gerritt had, so he added, "But we can take a really careful look at all the stone walls down here, maybe see if there's a hidden door somewhere else. That makes sense, don't you think?"

Robert was already out of the shed, doing just that.

Ben began snapping pictures of the water wheel. He loved the way it was put together, such simplicity and strength. And, really, the only parts of the wheel that were damaged were the bucket-like blades, the parts that had dipped down to catch the flowing water of the millrace. The hub was still solid, and so were all the spokes and the outer rim of the wheel. The thing had to weigh half a ton. It was nearly ten feet in diameter, from the bottom blades two feet below the floor level, to the topmost ones that almost scraped the ceiling.

And the workmanship was great. He focused in tightly on one of the broad spokes and snapped a picture of the wood, noticing the marks left by a tool—which had probably been held by John Vining himself. He snapped again and focused on a place closer to the outer rim, marveling at how tightly everything was joined together . . . and then he saw something, carefully carved into the oak—one word about an inch tall, just two letters: "in"!

And beside the word, a triangle—a pointer!

He leaned out into the center space of the wheel, holding on to the door frame of the shed. Using his headlamp beam, he slowly scanned the boards on the outer wall of the shed, as far as he could see on the left side of the doorway's opening . . . nothing. Then he did it again on the right side. And this time he saw it, much harder to spot because the old pine boards of the shed were a lot darker than the oak of the wheel.

But there it was, the same word with the same pointer . . . except this pointer was aimed at the opposite direction!

"Hey, Jill, Robert! Come help me turn the big wheel!"

Robert snorted from twenty feet away. "Give it up, Pratt. Let's get out of this dungeon."

"Gerritt, I'm serious—I found something! Come look!"

The tone of Ben's voice got both Jill and Robert to the doorway in seconds.

"See the words?" Ben said, aiming the beam of his headlamp. "'In'! A man walks *in*! It has to be linked to the clue, so we've got to get these two pointers to line up!"

Robert said, "You stay here, and I'll go see if I can move the wheel from the front—that should give me enough leverage."

He went out of the shed and then around to the leading edge of the wheel, the part facing east. Ben could see his headlamp shining between the wheel and the side of the shed.

"Okay, here goes."

Robert pulled down with his whole weight, and instantly the wheel spun smoothly, almost half a turn—the hub didn't even squeak on the axle.

"Easy," called Ben. "Too far. Bring it back up about a foot . . . slowly . . . a little more . . . stop!"

The two pointers were lined up perfectly.

Jill whispered, "Do you see that?"

"I sure do," said Ben.

There were actually two things staring them in the face.

First, with the pointers lined up, a square notch in the outer rim of the wheel lined up with a square post that was set into a granite block on the wall beyond. The post had an iron ring on its end, and when Ben pulled on the ring, the post slid out of the rock about eight inches, just far enough to fit into the matching notch on the wheel—which meant the wheel was now locked in place.

Gerritt was beside them again, and he saw the second thing instantly. "Check it out—that's a walkway!"

And it was—sort of a short footbridge right through the wheel. With the water wheel locked in this exact position, an opening among the spokes lined up directly in front of the doorway from the shed, complete with boards to step on.

But the little path went nowhere. Beyond the outer edge of the wheel there was nothing but solid granite, the rough blocks of the northern foundation wall.

"You think it's safe to walk on?" asked Jill.

Ben said, "Should be—here, hold on and give it a try."

He held out a hand. She took it and then stepped out onto the boards. The wheel moved a little, but the square block locking it in place held tight.

"Feels pretty solid," she said.

"Good," said Ben, and he let go of her hand. He reached down and picked up a hefty piece of rounded oak, a tooth that had broken off one of the wooden millstone gears.

He passed it to Jill and said, "Give one of those granite blocks a good whack."

She did, and then gasped as a wide slab of rock tipped toward her. Except it wasn't rock— Ben knew that from the sound he'd heard when she'd hit it. It was a wooden panel, carved and painted to look like the rest of the wall!

He stepped forward and stood next to Jill.

"You grab the left edge and I'll get this side. . . . Okay, now lower it to the ground."

They both had to lean down, because the floor was a good six feet below the platform they stood on. Ben decided the panel must be made of pine—it didn't weigh very much.

They straightened up and aimed their headlamps where the panel had been, and Ben knew exactly what they were looking at.

It was a door.

CHAPTER 11

Indiana Pratt

This was not a normal door. Anyone could tell that much.

But Ben needed a closer look, and Jill was in front of him again, blocking part of his view.

"Um, could we swap places for a second?"

"Yeah, Jill," Robert said. "Move aside and let Indiana Pratt come to the rescue."

Another wisecrack. Gerritt was pushing hard today, and it was very distracting. Ben was almost sure it was because of that business with Wally before school—he was going to have to find a way to bring that up . . .

"No problem," said Jill, and Ben snapped back

into the moment. She stepped aside and slipped past him on the narrow walkway.

Up close with his headlamp on full power, Ben confirmed what he'd thought: The door was covered with copper—several large, overlapping sheets. The metal had turned a mottled green. Oxidation—that's what Mr. Collins would call it.

Similar to the wooden hatchway Robert had opened, this door also had an iron ring lying flat, set into its surface. Ben worked the ring out far enough to get both hands around it and pulled. . . . Nothing, no give at all.

And that's when he saw the wire—a twisted loop of wire at the upper left-hand corner of the door frame.

"Hey, guys!" he called. "Remember the pictures I took of that little brass coffin lid last week? The edges of this door are sealed shut exactly the same way!"

He snapped four quick photos. The wire was embedded in pine pitch that had been pushed into the crack between the door and the granite blocks surrounding it. Putting his index finger through the twisted wire, he pulled. It ripped through the brittle resin all around the door frame, and dark chips flew off in all directions.

Ben dropped the wire, grabbed the ring on the door, and yanked at it again. There was a little movement this time, but just a fraction of an inch. He felt footsteps behind him, and then Robert's light was on the door, too, scanning the edges.

"You're pulling the wrong way, Pratt. The door doesn't open out—or in either. It slides to the right. . . . See those scrape marks?"

Ben pulled sideways on the ring, and the door slid smoothly, gliding into a slot built into the wall. Then he squeezed to the left and said, "You figured it out, Gerritt—you should go in first."

Robert grinned. "Yeah, that way *I'm* the one who gets an axe in the neck from the booby trap, right?"

Robert went ahead anyway. Ben was right behind him, and Jill followed them both. All three stood still, just inside the doorway, not saying a word, their headlamp beams darting around the space as they tried to take it all in.

The first thing Ben saw was a massive ship's wheel—actually, a *double* wheel with a wide cylinder in between! It stood in the corner to the left of the doorway, held up by a stand that looked like it had been ripped right off the quarterdeck of a warship. And as he looked at that wooden stand, he noticed the beautiful red-and-blue oriental rug it rested on— the floor of the whole room was nearly covered with thick, rich carpets! The room itself was fairly large, probably twenty feet by thirty feet, and the low ceiling was held up by a dozen sturdy wooden posts.

Jill said, "Can you believe this place? It's like a museum!"

Ben walked to a square table with raised edges that stood in the center of the room. "This is a chart table—and these maps? They're probably the ones the captain actually used!"

He aimed his phone's camera and took a quick picture of the map on top—it was Barclay Bay, and there on the shoreline of Edgeport, he saw that the captain's building had been circled with black ink. Ben wanted to look at every single chart, but there were too many other things to see.

Walking to the back of the room, he found a round table with six chairs. There was a full set of sterling silver dining dishes, two candlesticks, plus six goblets and six sets of silverware, all laid out—every piece tarnished completely black, but heavy, and covered with rich engravings. It

was like the captain was expecting to entertain visitors . . . and then it struck Ben.

"Guys, guys! This whole room? It was made to look like the captain's cabin on a ship! See the bunk over there, with the board along the side? That was to keep someone from rolling out of bed when the waves were rough. And that hanging brass lamp, and the chart table with the raised sides? Just like in a captain's cabin! And check out the cabinet with the pistols and swords and muskets—all that stuff was kept locked up in the

captain's quarters until right before a battle!"

Robert had just opened another glass-fronted cabinet, and he gave a low whistle. "Old Man Oakes brought his whole library down here! Here's a huge Bible . . . and a ton of books about navigation and shipbuilding. There's a poetry section, and folded maps . . . and all kinds of science books about plants and animals and fish. And a bunch more about astronomy . . . and Shakespeare's plays, too! These are probably worth *millions*!"

Ben lifted the lid of a brass-strapped sea

chest and found more books, dozens of leather-bound volumes. He carefully opened one and saw neat, precise handwriting on every page. He was holding the ship's log for a voyage of a ship called *The Anne*, which had sailed from Edgeport for London on April 3, 1762. Captain Oakes had written out the names of all the officers and crew, and he'd recorded a complete list of the cargo. Page after page, there were calculations of the ship's position, which stars had been visible in the night sky, the daily weather reports, and the distance the ship had traveled from noon to noon, day by day—all the way from Edgeport to the docks in London on the Thames River. The voyage had taken seventy-seven days—over two and a half months!

Ben closed the log and put it back in the chest. He was about to pull out another one, when he noticed something. There was no carpet under the sea chest, so he could see the floor. And it was covered with copper! He took three steps and lifted the edge of a rug—underneath was also copper, and unlike the greenish copper that had covered the outer door, in here all the metal was that rich, orange-brown color of an old penny. Then he aimed his light at the ceiling, and at the wall behind the dining table. The entire room had been encased with copper sheets, with every edge sealed together with melted lead! And in a flash, Ben knew exactly why: This room had been designed to stay *dry*!

The copper lining had done its job perfectly. Even though this space was deep underground and only fifty feet from the ocean, the room and everything in it had been completely protected from dampness and decay for more than two hundred years. If anything, the room felt dry and dusty—more like an attic than a basement.

"Here's the whole Oakes family!" called Jill.

Ben shut the sea chest and went to look. Jill was peering at six miniatures, small framed portraits arranged on the wall beside the bunk. The pictures had been painted on three-inch ovals that looked like ivory: Captain Oakes, his wife, and four children— three boys and a girl. Everyone looked stiff and formal in their fanciest clothes.

"And look at *this*!" Robert said. "It's like a cash register!"

In a deep drawer below the gun cabinet, Ben saw several hundred gold and silver coins. *"Yow!"*

he whispered. "That is some *serious* dough!"

Two thick blocks of pine ran the full width of the drawer, and along the outer edges of both blocks, a row of holes had been bored into the wood—holes just the right diameter and depth to fit a tall stack of coins.

Ben said, "I wonder if those—"

But Jill interrupted. "What *I* wonder is *this*: Is anything we've seen in here going to make a difference when it comes to actually *stopping* the Glennley plan? The weapons and the books and stuff—it's all amazing, and the historical importance is completely crazy, not to mention what everything's worth. But here's the important question: Will any of it really *help*?" She paused a moment, then said, "And I say *no*. None of this stuff is going to matter one bit. Not the documents, not the artifacts, not the place itself. Remember what happened after we found the Underground Railroad station, and we were so sure that it would be enough to make the building a national landmark? Glennley completely robbed us, and they'll try to do the same thing here— they'll figure out a way to blend all of this into their amusement park. I just don't think *any* of this can be turned into a real weapon that we can *use*."

Robert said, "So, like, what should we do about this place—*nothing*? Is *that* what you're saying?"

Ben winced. Gerritt sounded like he was talking to a two-year-old—and Jill reacted.

"You know what, Robert?" she snapped. "You're about ninety-nine percent *jerk* most of the time, and I've learned how to deal with that. But when you go and turn yourself into a *complete* rump, it's too much! I am *not* saying we do nothing! We take a ton of pictures, and then we close this place up again so Lyman and Wally can't find it. And then we get prepared to *use* all those pictures, along with all our other last-minute stuff, like the codicil. And if we need to, we release the pictures to the media, and Twitter, and YouTube, and the newspapers, and the governor's office, and the state historical commission, and everywhere else we can think of—and that'll *have* to help to stop the wrecking crew, even if it's only for a day or two. But now? Right *now*, we have to go for the big knockout punch. We need get out of here, regroup, and go find that last safeguard—and we have to hope that it's not just another collection of antiques."

Jill stopped and took a breath. "So that's my

proposal. And I'm putting it to a vote, right now. All in favor of doing what I just said, raise your hand."

Robert said, "But . . ."

Jill glared at him. "I *said*, all in favor, raise your hand."

The decision was unanimous.

The next half hour was a blur. Everything they could find was photographed, and they were all half blind from the constant flashes of Robert's good camera. There seemed to be no end to the treasures.

Ben found two chronometers, a massive ship's compass, and three brass telescopes. Along with the cutlasses and muskets and pistols, there were a dozen heavy boarding axes, the kind sailors swung left and right when attacking the deck of an enemy ship. And in a drawer below the bunk bed, he found a matched pair of dueling pistols in a wooden box lined with blood-red velvet.

In one corner there was a small oak barrel, and at first Ben thought it must be wine, or maybe rum. The stopper on top was loose, and he pulled it out and took a sniff.

"Hey!" he called. "Check it out—a keg of gunpowder!" And instantly he realized that the *first* reason this room had been lined with copper wasn't to keep moisture away from the captain's books and papers—they had stored the gunpowder from the mill in here!

In a tall wardrobe Jill found Captain Oakes's uniform: hat, coat, white breeches, and tall leather boots, plus a heavy blue woolen overcoat—even a wig and fine leather gloves. Ben pictured the captain on the deck of a ship during an Atlantic passage, his face into the wind as he swept the horizon with a telescope, on the lookout for an enemy sail.

And in a drawer inside the wardrobe, Jill also found a gold pocket watch, a wedding ring, and a stunning diamond necklace—the same one the captain's wife was wearing when her miniature portrait was painted!

Robert snapped shot after shot.

"Okay," Jill announced, "we have to stop now. There's a lot more, but we've got to get going."

Ben hated to quit—there were still drawers and little chests and cabinets that no one had even touched. But he knew Jill was right.

Robert didn't need convincing. "Yeah, let's go. It's all cool, but enough is enough."

They took a few minutes and made sure everything was just as they'd found it.

Jill said, "I think that's good. Ready?" She started for the door.

Ben said, "Looks right to me," but then he had an idea.

"Hey, Robert, can you set up that camera so it'll take a picture of the three of us, maybe here in front of the swords?"

"Sure," Robert said.

He fiddled with the controls and then set the camera on the corner of the chart table. He checked the display screen.

"You two stand there. Jill, a little to your left . . . good."

He pushed a button, and the camera started to beep as he hurried over and stood beside Ben.

Ben looked at the camera. As it kept beeping, he remembered what Robert had called him earlier: Indiana Pratt.

I wish I had one of those cool hats. . . .

And that thought made him smile—just as the camera flashed.

CHAPTER 12

Up and Out and Now

Hiding the door to the captain's secret cabin was pretty simple, just a matter of retracing each step. The copper door was slid shut, and Jill and Ben fitted the fake granite panel back into place. Then the block that kept the water wheel from moving was slid back into its slot, and the door on the wall of the mill shed was closed and fastened with the bent nail. Ben went outside the mill and turned the paddle wheel about half a revolution, and that was all it took. Jill found a worn-out broom in a corner and used it to swish the dust around, hiding their footsteps to and from the doorway. And Robert took at least a dozen pictures, documenting the whole process.

Getting up to the basement level and closing off the sub-basement was the same deal—reversing every step, slowly and carefully. The hinges and the chains of the heavy trap door squeaked and groaned as they lowered it, and Ben was afraid that any second Lyman or Wally would flip on the lights and come charging down the stairs from the janitor's workroom. But that didn't happen, and in a few minutes the entry was concealed, and this time, it was Robert who made sure that the area around the trap door looked undisturbed.

Ben tapped his tongue against the back of his teeth as they tiptoed toward the steps—something he did when he got nervous.

"Now comes the hard part—" Ben whispered, "getting outside without being caught. Headlamps off. We have to be really quiet now."

Gerritt rolled his eyes at that, and he also mouthed something—it took a second for Ben to figure out the word his lips had formed: *Duh*.

As worried as Ben was about getting out safely, Gerritt's attitude grabbed all his attention again.

What's up with him?

Because just yesterday afternoon Robert had said how these few weeks had been so great for him. It had seemed like he was being sincere, but there was no way to tell that from the way he was acting today.

I'm just gonna have to confront him, ask what Wally said this morning—get everything out in the open . . .

About twenty feet from the steps up to the janitor's room, Jill grabbed his arm and all three of them stopped short.

"What's that?" she whispered.

It sounded like a low rumble of thunder.

Robert said, "Relax—it's the trash bin rolling along the first-floor hallway."

At least he didn't say "duh," Ben thought.

But it was still there in the tone of his voice.

They heard the cart roll above their heads, then slow down and take a turn. Ben was pretty sure he heard the door to the janitor's room slam closed.

"We'd better back up a little way," Robert whispered. "We might be here awhile."

When they were a safe distance from the steps,

Jill said, "Anybody know when they usually leave the building?"

"No idea," said Robert.

Now he sounded bored.

Ben pulled out his cell phone to check the time, but as he did, it gave a sharp buzz in his hand.

"Cool—I just got signal again! And I've got two messages from ghost phone number five—that's Gabe."

Jill also had her phone out. "Yeah, me too—same message twice: 'Where are you guys?'"

Ben started to punch in a reply, when Jill gasped, "Stop! Don't answer him!" And she reached over and snatched Ben's phone.

"Hey, give me that!"

"Shh!" Jill said, and held it out of his reach. "Listen, I *also* got a text from phone number six—that's Luke, right?"

"So?" said Ben, still holding out his hand.

"So, Luke's text was sent *before* those two from Gabe, and it says, 'I'm on the bus, and Gabe just told me he left his phone in the gym.' So . . ."

"So . . . ," said Robert slowly, "Lyman or Wally must have found Gabe's phone . . . and then turned it on to see who it belonged to, and then saw those texts about *them*, when we asked if anyone knew where the janitors were!"

"Oh, great," Ben said. "*That* means our new communication system is trashed!"

"Wrong again, professor," Robert said. He was grinning now. "It *means* that we just got a free pass right out of here. Here, let me have Pratt's phone."

Jill handed it to him, and Robert said the words slowly as he typed them onto the screen.

> We're over on the north side of the school, hiding in the library. Have to go now. Big stuff happening.

Before Ben or Jill had fully processed what he was doing, Robert hit the send button.

Almost instantly, the door of the janitor's room banged open above them, and they heard heavy footsteps clomping down the hallway toward the office.

Robert handed Ben his phone. "And *that*, boys and girls, is how you clear the deck for a speedy escape from the Oakes School dungeon—let's go!"

Gerritt led the way, and in less than a minute

the three of them were up the steps, through the janitor's room, out the loading dock door, and then over the asphalt and running across the green parkland behind the school.

When they were almost to School Street, Ben stopped and dropped to his knees. "Too hot—I have to rest!"

The others flopped to the ground too, all three of them panting like dogs. It was at least ninety degrees outside—a sharp contrast with the cool basement.

Ben lay back, looking up into the swaying canopy of a big sugar maple. Any other year, he'd have been so happy on an afternoon like this—school nearly over, homework and tests all done, nothing to do but swim and sail and hang out by the harbor—at least until his mom and dad got him started on the summer chores.

But the end of school *this* year? It was so different.

Everything was different.

And with his parents separated, this whole summer was messed up.

He tried to find a word for the way he was feeling.

Sad? Yes, but it was more than that.

Angry? A little. More like a *lot*, at least sometimes.

Tired? Definitely some of that.

Then it struck him.

I'm feeling . . . old!

It seemed crazy, but that was how he felt: old. Maybe it was because everything seemed so heavy—like the feeling he'd had down in that sub-basement. Except now it wasn't the weight of the earth pressing in on him. It was the past—feeling responsible for saving all of it, for protecting it.

The past was crushing him—and the future felt even heavier.

His next thought shocked him.

Maybe the old school really should go, like Robert said during the fake debate—out with the old, in with the new. Let the future come as fast and nasty as it wants to. There's nothing in the past you can really count on anyway—and you can't trust the future either. You can't trust anything or anybody, not ever.

Almost as fast, another thought burst in—a big, loud *No!*

Ben knew all that negative stuff wasn't true. Because his mom was still his mom, and his dad was still his dad, and he knew he could *absolutely* trust each of them, no matter what.

So . . . what's my real problem? What do I actually want?

It was the third time today he'd asked himself that question.

An answer came—weird, but still, it was an answer, and it felt true.

I want the past and the future to shut up and leave me alone—I want to think about now.

Just as quickly, another challenge.

So, what's stopping you?

Ben shut his eyes and tried to get his mind around that—no past, no future, only now.

Patches of sunlight fluttered across his eyelids, and he smelled the salt of the ocean. Grass tickled the back of his neck, and the warm breeze brushed his arms and cheek. Along with rustling leaves and the cries of seagulls, he could hear Jill and Robert breathing only a few feet away.

He had to admit it—shut out all the other stuff, and now felt pretty good.

And deep down, a tiny part of his mind also admitted that hanging around with Jill was a pretty big part of what made *now* feel good.

And, yeah, it was good that Gerritt was here too—he was part of the new now. He just wasn't as big a part of what made it feel good.

Ben smiled.

The new now.

He liked the sound of it.

And this new now wasn't over, not *nearly* over!

There was stuff that all three of them needed to do, together. Now.

Because they had to, right?

Right!

Ben got to his feet.

"We'd better get going, guys."

He reached a hand and pulled Robert up, then did the same for Jill.

"We've still got a lot to do."

"Yeah? Like *what?*" asked Gerritt.

That tone again. But Ben didn't react.

He said, "Well, for starters, before I walk to the marina, I'm gonna stop at my mom's house and play with my dog a few minutes—want to come?"

Instantly, Jill said, "I do!"

Gerritt smiled—he tried not to, but he couldn't help himself.

"Yeah," he said, "why not? Nelson's the only

dog on this planet that I actually like."

Four minutes later when Nelson burst out of the kitchen door in a tail-wagging frenzy, Ben watched Jill and Robert laugh and hoot as they tried to catch him.

It was the best chunk of now that he'd seen all day long.

CHAPTER 13

Sinkhole

A quick look around Tom Benton's living room told Ben that he and his dad were the last to arrive. Tom had set up a few folding chairs, and Ben wasn't surprised to see that there was a table loaded with snacks over near the big windows that faced Barclay Bay—the old guy was crazy about fresh fruit. There was also a tall chocolate cake on the table too, probably brought by Mrs. Keane—at least he hoped so.

The air conditioner in a side window was making a lot of noise, but the room was still very warm. The only person who didn't look hot was Robert's grandmother. Ben was glad to see her, glad that Gerritt had brought her on board. It was a good sign that the guy just might be a human.

About two hours ago Jill had told him about this meeting—it had been her idea. "Everything depends on the next day or so, and we all have to be on the same page. And the best way to make that happen is to have a meeting. And you're in charge of running it."

That's what she'd said.

So he'd only had a couple hours to dread it and fret about it—which was plenty of time to get his stomach tied up in knots, and in spite of how hot it was as he and his dad had walked over from the marina, his hands felt cold and clammy.

But looking around the room now, he felt a little better. First off, it wasn't a very big group: Jill and Robert, Tom Benton, Mrs. Keane, Robert's grandmother, Jill's parents, his mom and dad, and the lawyer, Harold Chamden—ten people, not counting himself.

Then Ben recalled that quite a few others were missing: Arthur Rydens from the bank, the seven kids he had recruited during social studies today, and also Mrs. Hinman. So, including himself, that made . . . twenty—twenty Keepers of the School!

He remembered how alone he had felt the day Mr. Keane had died, leaving him totally responsible for trying to save the school.

This was *tons* better!

His dad walked over and sat near his mom, and he wished he could do the same. But Jill caught his eye and gave him a look that said, *Well? Get on with it!*

Ben cleared his throat and looked down at the items he'd written on an index card. The list was very short.

"Um . . . hi, everybody. We should get started. First, I want to ask Robert to tell about what we found down in the sub-basement of the school today, when we found the fourth safeguard."

Just that quickly, Ben realized that being in charge of a meeting wasn't so bad after all—you got to tell others to do stuff.

Ben watched how different people reacted as Gerritt gave a short summary of their expedition, holding up his iPad now and then to show pictures of all the discoveries. His grandmother looked so proud of him, and it was obvious that everyone was impressed with his clear explanations—even Jill.

The lawyer, Mr. Chamden, was scribbling

notes as fast as he could on a long yellow pad, and when Robert stopped, he had the first question.

"Can you e-mail me files of all those images, and a short explanation of where the objects are located?"

Robert nodded. "All set with that."

Mrs. Keane raised her hand, and when Ben pointed at her, she spoke to the lawyer.

"But won't all those wonderful things the children have found stop the developer? How could they still have the right to tear down the building?"

The lawyer said, "Well, it's probably just like the situation with the Underground Railroad hideout. Legally, the Glennley Group already has a very strong claim on the entire property, and as long as they act to preserve historically important elements, they'll most likely be allowed to proceed with their plans." He shrugged. "We'll just have to make our best case to a judge and see what happens."

That seemed to stun the group a little, and Ben felt like he should move to something more cheerful. So he asked the lawyer, "Has there been progress with the real estate stuff?"

Mr. Chamden smiled broadly. "Absolutely! We've put the Glennley Realty Group almost out of business up and down the coast. All the sellers were very happy to get better offers, and they're glad to be dealing with local people, too. This is going to take a big bite from the profits Glennley planned on, and it's also going save a lot of shoreline from overdevelopment." He shrugged again. "Of course, I'm not saying that this is going to make Glennley back away from the deal. They'll still make plenty of money from the theme park."

Another murmur of concern rippled through the group, and again Ben wanted to lighten things up.

He smiled around the room and said, "Um . . . well, the good news is . . ." But then he couldn't think of anything, not *really* good news. So he said, ". . . well, we have a whole day and a half to find the captain's last safeguard, and I forgot to mention that we recruited seven new kids today to help us out, and our social studies teacher, too, Mrs. Hinman. Plus, let's not forget that there's a chocolate cake and two huge bowls of fruit over there." That got a little laugh, but it didn't last long.

Ben asked, "Does anyone else have news? Or

ideas about steps we can take during the next day and a half? Or . . . anything?"

Jill's mom stood up.

"Well, *I* think we should launch a huge public relations attack against Glennley—send out everything we have about their fake janitors and the shameful way they stole that Underground Railroad site. And we should also use the new will, plus tell all about these things the kids found today, which ought to get the preservation community excited again. We should throw everything at them at once, and get the whole region stirred up about this. The Glennley company has to care about its public image, right? So let's take the fight straight to them and make a big stink, and let's do it tomorrow, before it's too late! That's what I say!"

The lawyer looked like he wanted to answer her, but Robert spoke first—and Ben was glad that he began so respectfully. Jill was watching him with her eyes narrowed, and a fight right now between Gerritt and Jill was the last thing the other Keepers needed to see.

"We've been thinking about all that too, Mrs. Acton. And it's probably going to happen pretty much like you said—except not tomorrow." He flipped open his iPad and swiped quickly at the screen a few times. "Listen to what Captain Oakes said about the last safeguard—this is from the message about the clues for the safeguards, which was the first thing that Ben and Jill found: 'Above all, seek the final safeguard ONLY IF YOU MUST—for once the last is found, our school will change forever.' So this last safeguard? It's probably something pretty special—the captain sure seems to think so. And before we hand everything over to some judge and all the Glennley lawyers to fight about, we've still got some time inside the school building. And we want to use that time and give it our best shot."

The lawyer wanted the last word. He stood up and slowly looked around, and Ben could picture him standing in a courtroom, delivering the final argument of a trial.

"No matter what might be found, and regardless of all the documents and evidence that we submit to the legal system or to the larger court of public opinion, there is still a very strong possibility that the Glennley position is just too strong and too well protected. To be completely honest, at this point, I cannot imagine what could fully stop their plans for the theme park. And I wouldn't be doing my job properly if I didn't prepare each of you for the distinct possibility that all our work may well come to nothing. . . . I'm sorry, but those are the facts . . . as I see them . . . at this moment."

Mr. Chamden sat down, and in the silence, Ben felt like the meeting had just slid sideways into a huge sinkhole, demolishing all their hope and optimism—a total loss. With the possible exception of the cake.

Help came from an unexpected source.

Robert's grandmother got to her feet. "I'm certainly not an expert on any of this. But I have to say that I am so pleased and impressed with everything that these young people have been doing—with all their spirit and initiative. And no matter what happens, a *lot* of good is going to come out of what they've done—I am completely sure of it!"

All the grown-ups jumped up and applauded, including the lawyer. And then Tom called out, "Well, how about we all have some food!"

The meeting was over.

Ben was right about the cake—Mrs. Keane

had brought it, and it tasted even better than the last time he'd eaten some.

But as good as the cake was, including the wonderful cold glass of milk he guzzled afterward, Ben still couldn't get the lawyer's last words out of his head: . . . *all our work may well come to nothing.*

CHAPTER 14

Jaws of the Beast

Tuesday looked like a beautiful June morning—
even though it was still uncomfortably warm and
humid. Bright sun, every tree in full leaf, and each
bush and flower around the schoolyard bursting
with color. Plus, Ben had decided that the kids
sitting on either side of him were turning out to
be real friends—and Jill might become more than
that . . . someday.

But none of that helped. Ben felt awful—all
of them did.

They sat on Captain Oakes's gravestone, silent

and grim, because they couldn't take their eyes off the diesel-drinking monster that had crept onto Washington Street during the night. Even though it was more than a hundred yards away, the size and power of the demolition machine still overwhelmed them.

He and Robert and Jill had met at school a half hour early so they could get a head start on the final safeguard search, but the destructive power of the huge contraption had hit them like a punch in the stomach. Walking slowly around the thing a while ago, it had reminded Ben of a huge trebuchet, one of those medieval war engines for smashing castles.

Mostly yellow, it had tractor treads over twenty feet long. The engine unit was as big as a dump truck, and it had a huge jointed neck that stretched more than sixty feet—it needed its own extra trailer. And at the end of that neck was a set of jaws that made it look like a mechanical dragon. The mouth of the beast had been spray painted a bloody red—somebody's idea of a joke. Bright metal glinted where the steel teeth had been polished by chewing on concrete and brick.

Ben recalled the nightmare he'd had about the death of the school—he had dreamed of a wrecking ball bursting through the walls. Somehow, this seemed worse, to have giant jaws crunching the place to bits. And the grin on the thing? It reminded him of Lyman's smile.

That thought had an effect on Ben. It made him

mad—and that sharp burst of anger woke him up.

"Hey," he said, "that thing's nothing but a pile of junk chained to a trailer, right? And it can roll away from here just the way it came. So let's stay focused, okay?"

His voice sounded hollow, as if he didn't believe his own words.

He tried again, putting his heart into it.

"And don't forget the codicil, and the pictures from the underground room, and all the other last-minute stuff we've got cooking. Come on, guys, we can't wimp out now. 'After one still star, horizons afar'—that's what we need to think about. This is a big day for us—it's our star search day! There's not

really time before homeroom now, but at least we can show Wally and Lyman that we haven't given up. Let's show 'em that we still own this place!"

Jill moved first. She turned away from the big machine and stood up.

"Yeah," she said, "no point in sitting here like monkeys on an island. Let's go, Robert."

Robert stayed put. "I don't need a cheerleader to tell me what I should do, and I'll sit here on my island as long as I want to. So why don't you shut up—and go fetch me a banana."

It was more of that same surly attitude—which had gotten much worse since Gerritt's run-in with Wally yesterday morning.

Ben was afraid Jill was going to explode, and when she turned and took a step toward Robert, he expected the worst. But she looked over at Ben with a devilish smile and said, "You know what monkeys like more than bananas? They like to play . . . chase the bag!" And without warning she grabbed Robert's backpack and jumped to the ground.

"C'mon, Ben, let's play catch!"

Ben hopped down, and Jill tossed him the backpack.

"Hey!" Robert shouted. "The good camera's in there!"

Jill hooted like a chimp, and said, "Me doesn't understand!"

"You are *dead*," Robert yelled, scrambling to his feet. "Do you understand *that*?"

Jill grabbed the backpack from Ben and took off toward the front of the school. "Big words, banana brain," she called over her shoulder. "Let's see if you're monkey enough to catch me!"

Robert leapt off the gravestone, and as he went past Ben, he landed a fist on his shoulder.

Ben winced, but then he grinned and said, "Not bad, for a monkey!"

Gerritt stopped short. "Yeah? Well, here comes another one!"

But Ben was ready, and he dodged the next punch, and he also saw that Robert smiled a little—it was all pretty stupid.

Ben backed away, so Robert turned and started toward the front of the school. But then Ben called, "Hey, Gerritt—hang on a second. I've gotta tell you something."

Gerritt stopped again and turned to face him, defiant. "Yeah? *What?*"

Ben almost chickened out, almost said, *Forget it*. But he walked toward Gerritt and made himself keep talking. "Yesterday, before school? I was hiding in the bushes along the path toward the Annex—I was gonna to jump out and scare you, just a goofy prank."

Ben saw a quick ripple of thought cross Robert's face as the memory came back.

Gerritt looked him in the eye. "So . . . you saw Wally, too, right?"

Ben nodded. "Yeah, and I saw you shove right past him—which was *awesome!*" He paused, waiting for the explanation, but Robert didn't seem like he was going to say anything.

Ben went on, "So . . . what did Wally say to you?"

Robert looked down and shrugged. "Just a bunch of garbage. He said *I* should team up with *him*—can you believe that? He said Lyman didn't really trust him. And he said—" Gerritt stopped, and then looked Ben straight in the eye again. "He . . . he said Lyman doesn't really trust *him*—the same way that you and Jill don't really trust *me*."

Ben's mouth dropped open. "He said *that*? What a *creep*! That's the stupidest thing I've ever heard! I mean . . . you *know* how crazy that is, right?"

"Oh . . . yeah—of course!" said Gerritt. "Completely nuts!"

But Ben heard the pause, a tiny fraction of a second. Because Wally's attack had hit a weak spot.

Ben didn't break eye contact. "Listen, Robert. That is *total* junk. I mean, you're . . . you're like my brother—really. And if it wasn't for you? Me and Jill—we'd be sunk most of the time! And I *also* heard what you yelled at Wally, and you were right—that idiot doesn't know *anything*!"

Robert smiled a little. "Your brother, huh?"

"Yeah," said Ben, "who I would trust with my life—my smarter, grumpier, incredibly annoying little brother!"

Gerritt laughed and acted like he was going to whack Ben's arm again, but held up at the last second.

"Hey, monkey boys!"

It was Jill, yelling at them from the front corner of the school and waving Robert's book bag. "You gonna hang around outside all day or what?"

Gerritt took off after her, and Ben followed.

When they rounded the corner, Jill was gone and Robert's backpack was sitting on the steps by the front door. They both started to dig for their hall passes, but Mrs. Hendon waved from the office window and buzzed them in just as the first entry bell clanged.

Ben followed Gerritt into the front hall, and immediately their mood changed. It was time to get back to business.

Ugh.

It felt at least ten degrees hotter inside the school. He wanted to turn around and go right back out the door. But this building was the battlefield, and they were just going to have to deal with the heat.

Ben pointed to his right. "I'm heading for homeroom—you going that way?"

"Yeah," Robert said, "I've got to take a book to the library."

They started walking, and Ben could tell that the tension between them was gone now. It felt good.

Just past the nurse's office, Ben stopped and stared up at the old map of colonial Edgeport. Robert stopped too.

After about ten seconds, Gerritt said, "Nice try, Pratt, but there are no stars on that thing. I gotta get to the library or I'll be late for homeroom." He walked away, but Ben stayed put.

Gerritt had guessed right—Ben *was* looking for stars. This seemed as good a place as any to start solving the final clue. And he stood there until the homeroom warning bell ran, studying every square inch of the large drawing.

But Robert had been correct—annoyingly correct. There wasn't a single star to be seen.

So . . . does being that smart mean he can actually see *that much faster?*

Ben shrugged. Nothing about Gerritt surprised him anymore.

Trudging past the library and then turning south, Ben realized that he'd have a view of the demolition tractor from the windows of the art room. Not a happy thought, so he aimed his mind back to the problem at hand.

After one still star, horizons afar. . . .

The heat, the humidity, and the feeling that time was running out—it was a bad combination. This was their last full day of school, they had one clue left to solve, and even if they solved it and found that final safeguard, there was no way to know if it would be enough to save the school.

And the harbor.

And the town.

Ben had studied some of history's great battles, and the winning side usually had plenty of resources, capable leaders, and a strong plan of attack.

Resources?

Yes, they had good communications, loads of money, and a full team of intelligence agents and allies—inside and outside the school.

Capable leaders?

Yes . . . mostly. He and Jill and Gerritt had proven that they could solve problems and react quickly to changing conditions.

A strong plan of attack?

No. Not today.

And that was the problem.

Because wandering around a big old building, looking for something about a star? *That* wasn't the kind of plan that would win a battle.

Really, it wasn't a plan at all.

CHAPTER 15

Tug-of-War

Ben didn't look out the south-facing windows during homeroom. But all the other kids did.

"Cool! Check out the *jaws* on that thing!"

"I bet it's gonna rip this place down in ten minutes!"

"Yeah, me an' Tommy climbed all over it last night—even inside the control cab!"

"Seriously, that thing *rules*!"

All the tall windows in the art room were wide open, but the heat was still awful. At eight o'clock it was already close to eighty-five degrees— probably even hotter up on the second and third floors.

A text buzzed his phone . . . from Gerritt, and it had also been sent to Jill:

Afer one still star . . . that might be the north star, right?

It was a good idea . . . smart, as usual. Not that it was going to make the search any easier. But Ben replied to both Gerritt and Jill.

Yeah, good point.
Anybody spotted L or W?

Jill replied:

L n W in auditorium—putting up risers for concert tonite
BTW, I gave a new phone to old #5—now #9.

Then Gerritt added:

Also BTW, I txtd a joke to W on old #5 phone, then blocked all future calls from him, which everybody should do—go to Settings, Block Contact—spread the word!

Gerritt texted a joke to Wally? Ben couldn't resist.

What was the joke?

Gerritt wrote:

It went back and forth, me first—
Knock, knock.
Who's there?
Wally.
Wally who?
Wally who ain't so bright!
—L8r

Ben smiled as he put his phone away. Texting with Gerritt was a lot more fun than being in the same room with him.

The bell clanged for morning announcements, and after a fourth grader led the Pledge, Mr. Telmer took over on the intercom, all business.

"This is an important piece of news, so please pay careful attention. Because of the extreme heat and humidity in the weather forecast, I have instructed the staff to move all regular classes outdoors onto the school grounds today. Lunches will be in the cafeteria as usual, and we'll follow the normal bell schedule. I'm sure this is going to cause some problems, but it still seems like the best plan under these circumstances. Also, the school nurse is reminding all of us to drink plenty of water, to keep out of direct sunlight, and to avoid extra exercise. Since the auditorium has air conditioning, the after-school rehearsal for tonight's concert will go ahead as planned, and so will the concert. Thank you, and please have a safe and happy next-to-last day of school."

For half a second, Ben thought, Yay! Total goof-off day!

Then he remembered.

He and Jill and Robert really needed to be *inside*—it was now or never.

His phone buzzed—a text from Jill.

I'm on it

Huh?

But before he could reply to her, Ms. Wilton clapped her hands twice and said, "Listen up—all of my first-period art kids, come to the back of the room."

Three minutes later, as Ms. Wilton was loading him up with an armful of sketch pads to carry outside, Ben was surprised to see Jill walk in. She came straight to the art teacher and handed her a note.

Ms. Wilton read it, then reached over and took the stack of paper away from Ben.

"Sorry," she said, "you have to go work in the library."

By the time they were out in the hallway, Ben had put it together.

"You've got Hinman for homeroom!"

"Correct-o-matic, Mr. Pratt. And her note just asked the art lady if you could go work on a special project this period."

"Gerritt?"

"Same deal, except Mrs. Burmeister wanted him to stay and sit outside under a tree and actually work on math problems. But he won that argument."

Gerritt won an argument with the Mathmeister?

Ben was impressed.

Walking through the empty hallway with Jill, turning the corner toward the library, and then following her over to the alcove on the east wall—

everything felt so familiar, so *right*. This was where they'd found the codicil hidden under the bench . . . and there was the silver chronometer in its glass case on the wall, both hands pointing straight down— five bells. Ben couldn't believe that had happened less than a month ago . . . one month!

Time had been flying, zooming by incredibly fast!

He sat down on the bench and suddenly felt a little dizzy. He gripped the edge of the table in front of him with both hands.

That feeling he'd had lying on the grass yesterday afternoon, that feeling of *now*? It slammed into his head again, much stronger this time, a total certainty that NOW was so completely important.

At the same moment, he got a strong feeling that this *particular* now would never, ever come again.

Which wasn't really a sad feeling—it made him feel . . . free.

Yeah, free, because . . .

"Benjamin . . ." Jill was looking into his face, concerned.

"What . . . what's the matter?" he asked.

That's what he said out loud.

But he thought, Have her eyes always been blue like that?

She said, "You had a really weird look on your face—are you okay?"

He smiled and felt a blush start to creep up his neck. "Yeah . . . I'm totally okay."

And as the sounds came out of his mouth, he realized they just might be the truest words he had ever spoken.

But before he had a chance to enjoy the moment, Robert thumped his backpack onto the table and said, "Move over, Pratt, and prepare to be amazed."

They both looked at him.

Robert said, "Here's a crucial question: Who do you think is the smartest, the best informed, the brightest, the sharpest person in the whole school—other than me, I mean. Think hard, sir and madam. Because *I* think we have been missing out on a key ingredient, a vital ally and advisor, and this is a situation we need to fix. Immediately. Can you figure it out—the next-smartest individual in the whole school?"

Ben grinned. "You mean Lyman, right?"

That got him a dirty look.

"Guess again, wise guy."

But Ben didn't have to guess. He just looked at Jill.

From the expression on her face, it was clear that she knew, and all he had to do was follow her eyes.

Then he knew too.

And he remembered what every teacher since second grade had told him every time he had to do a book report, every time he had to finish a project, every time he needed to figure something out: *If you get stuck, you can always ask the librarian for help.*

Ben said, "Gerritt, I'm going to say this out loud only this one time, so you'd better enjoy it: *You* are a total *genius!*"

Gerritt smiled. "Yeah, I know. Let's go!"

Jill didn't move.

She frowned and said, "Um . . . I mean, I agree that Mrs. Sinclair's smart and everything, and she's been here at the school a long time—she might know some stuff that could help. But have you seen the plans for the library at the new school? It's pretty amazing, and I think she's really looking forward to the change. I'm not sure if we should tell her *everything*, unless we have to."

Robert shrugged. "Suit yourself—just an idea I had."

It was plain he was only pretending not to care.

Then with a flash of anger, he added, "And, as usual, you agree with *her*—right, *Pratt*?"

Ben almost lost it.

First of all, what about the talk they'd had less than half an hour ago, about trusting each other, about being like brothers? Had he forgotten *that*?

And secondly, he'd been in this spot too many times. Ben wanted to shout at Robert—really, at both of them: *Why does everything have to turn into a stupid tug-of-war—and how come I always end up feeling like the rope?*

And he thought, *No*, I am *not* doing this anymore!

Then, just as quickly, Ben knew that he *did* have to do this.

He *did* have to keep the peace, and keep everyone working together, and keep the whole effort moving forward. That was his job.

He took a deep breath and said, "You're both right. We *do* need all the help we can get, and Mrs. Sinclair might have some ideas—*but* she also might have strong feelings about moving on to the new school. So let's try Jill's way first—hold back the full story and see if we can get good information anyway."

Ben looked at each of them. "Okay?"

Neither liked his answer much, but Ben didn't care. Making them happy wasn't his job. His job was to try to save the school. And the harbor. And the town.

They each gave him a reluctant nod.

"Good. And, Jill, since it's your idea to start off cautiously, you do the talking."

"Fine," said Gerritt. "I'll just wait here." He pulled out his iPad and flipped open the cover.

Again, Ben nearly snapped. But he didn't.

"Sounds good, Gerritt—thanks."

And for that kind word, Robert gave him another incredibly annoying shrug.

But Ben didn't react. He got up and followed Jill toward the librarian's desk.

CHAPTER 16

The View from Above

Ben stood beside Jill at the front desk of the library.

So . . . was Jill feeling the same pressure he was? Because he felt like they really needed to show Gerritt that she could get something useful out of the librarian without telling her about the Keepers. Even though he'd meant that compliment about Gerritt being a total genius, and even though he truly liked and respected him, *somebody* still had to show the guy that he wasn't the absolute king of the universe . . . right?

Mrs. Sinclair looked up at them and smiled.

"May I help you with something?"

Jill said, "Well, I know this is kind of random, but can you think of anything around the school that has to do with stars?"

The librarian nodded. "There are quite a few books on . . ."

Jill shook her head. "No, I'm looking for something that might be part of the school building itself, like a carving on a bookcase or a door somewhere . . . or maybe a design you saw somewhere, something shaped like a star on the floor, or a wall . . . a ceiling somewhere . . . even on a doorknob. . . ."

Jill's voice trailed off, and Ben saw her start to blush, saw her realize that Mrs. Sinclair must be thinking how crazy she sounded.

But if the librarian was thinking that, she didn't show it.

"Hmm . . . let me think . . . something to do with stars. . . . No, I can't really picture anything like that. Can you be a little more specific?"

"Well, if there *was* something somewhere, it would have to be really old, something as old as Captain Oakes himself, something . . . about a star."

Again Jill looked embarrassed, but a thought lit up the librarian's face.

"Oh! I think I have something for you—this way!"

She turned left and walked briskly toward the east wall of library, then stopped just to the left of the alcove—very close to where Gerritt was sitting. He was still staring at his iPad, pretending not to notice them.

Mrs. Sinclair stopped and pointed. "There!"

Jill looked confused, and did Ben too. She was pointing at the big unabridged dictionary. It was lying open in front of her on its own sturdy little stand.

"The dictionary?" said Jill. "I don't see what—"

"No, not the book." Mrs. Sinclair said, and she quickly picked it up and set it on a shelf to the right. The dictionary had completely covered the thick glass top of a display case.

"See that?" she said, pointing into the case. "It's a navigation instrument called a sextant, and it was used by Captain Oakes. There aren't any star *shapes* here, or at least I don't think there are. But that telescope tube on top? I believe that was aimed at a star or sometimes at a planet. And after sighting the star, a navigator could adjust the tool and then read information from it to figure out a ship's location."

Two girls came into the library, each with a big stack of books. Mrs. Sinclair glanced at them and said, "I have to get back to the desk, but I hope this is useful."

Jill smiled and said, "Thanks—it might be just what we need."

Ben was pretty sure it wasn't. Still, the thing was interesting—and beautifully made. It was solid brass with hardly a speck of tarnish, nestled inside a wooden box lined with purple cloth. He had seen modern sextants on display at the

Clearwater Sailing Club, but even the newer ones were like antiques now. They weren't used much for navigation or location-fixing anymore—not since radio waves and satellite signals had solved those problems.

Jill grabbed his wrist, and the suddenness gave him a jolt.

She pointed, and whispered, "Read!"

Ben spotted the inscription. It was on a brass panel attached inside the lid of the box.

SEXTANT MADE BY JESSE RAMSDEN,
LONDON, 1763
WITH THIS INSTRUMENT AND ONE STILL STAR,
I SAFELY GUIDED MY SHIP
ACROSS THE ATLANTIC OCEAN SIXTEEN TIMES.
ONCE KEPT UNDER LOCK AND KEY IN MY CABIN,
NOW THAT I HAVE COME HOME FROM THE SEA,
IT RESTS HERE AS A REMINDER TO EACH CHILD:
SET A TRUE COURSE,
AND THEN CLIMB ALOFT AND KEEP A SHARP LOOKOUT.
DUNCAN OAKES, APRIL 12, 1791

One still star—the same words from the last clue! No way could that be a coincidence!

"And that date!" whispered Jill. "It's exactly the same as the date on the copper plate—where we found the list of clues!"

Ben's mind was racing, and Jill still had a grip on his wrist. He twisted his hand free, pulled out his phone, and snapped a picture of the small plaque.

"Quick," he said, "grab the dictionary and put it back on . . ."

Too late.

Lyman stood about five feet behind them, leaning against a bookcase and smiling, a toothpick sticking from the corner of his mouth. He pulled a dust cloth out of his back pocket and gave a swipe or two across the front of a shelf.

"You know," he said, "it's inspiring to see kids who get so excited about learning something new. It makes *me* want to learn new things too."

Jill turned a cold eye on him.

"Maybe you can learn to be a better liar," she said, "or a better spy—maybe even a better person someday, except I'm not holding my breath on that one, *Mr. Lyman.* But what would be really good right now, would be if you just went somewhere else and worked on being a better janitor, instead of following us around all the time. And if you don't leave *right now*, I am going to yell over to Mrs. Sinclair and tell her that you've been saying mean things to us."

While Jill was talking, Ben had turned away, his phone still in his hands.

Lyman kept smiling. "Well, *Miss Acton*, I think I'm going to call your bluff—I see quite a few messy fingerprints on that display case, and some dust, too. And when a man has work to do, then snotty little children need to move aside."

Lyman took a step forward, craning his neck to see what they'd been looking at.

Ben quickly turned, and he also stepped forward. He stood there, his arms folded, blocking Lyman's way. He felt a touch against his elbow— Gerritt was beside him, using his iPad as a video camera.

Robert said, "Hey, Mr. Lyman, can you give us a big I-work-for-the-Glennley-Group smile?"

"Step aside, boys." He held up his dust rag. "I have *work* to do here, and you're in my way." The smile was gone.

Ben shook his head. "You're gonna have to shove us. Or you could call to the librarian for help. Or the principal. Or maybe you could call your mommy, *Mr. Lyman*."

It was no fun being nose to nose with someone so deeply angry—this was a lot scarier than getting yelled at by the principal last week. Lyman's eyes narrowed to thin slits, and the man bit down so hard on the toothpick in his mouth that Ben heard it crack.

The intercom clanged, and Mrs. Hendon's voice called, "Mrs. Sinclair? Is Mr. Lyman in the library?"

Ben smiled, and he saw the man's face change as his name was spoken. Lyman broke eye contact and looked toward the front desk as the librarian replied.

"Yes, he's here, Rita."

"Please tell him to go up to the third floor right away—a sink overflowed in the girls' room, and his assistant isn't responding."

Gerritt's eyes never left the iPad screen, but he grinned and whispered to the image he was recording, "Bye-bye, Mr. Lyman."

The intercom went dead, and Mrs. Sinclair said, "I guess you heard all that, Jerry."

Lyman turned and headed toward the door. "Sure did. I'm on my way."

Ben heard the fake smile in his voice, and Lyman added, "It's sure going to be *great* when they knock this building down—it's time to put the old dump out of its misery!"

Ben knew that the janitor was talking to them, not Mrs. Sinclair, and as the library door hissed shut behind him, he wanted to shout, *Yeah, well we'll just see about* that . . . *Jerry!*

Gerritt had a different reaction.

He walked right to the librarian's desk, leaned forward, and said, "Do you agree with what Mr. Lyman just said, about tearing down the school? Do you?"

Mrs. Sinclair looked as if Robert had insulted her. "Of course not! It's a terrible idea, and that amusement park will *ruin* Edgeport!" Ben and Jill had come over and were standing there with Robert. She looked flustered and quickly glanced around to see if anyone else had noticed her outburst.

Mrs. Sinclair looked from face to face. "I . . . I didn't mean to be so emotional. Mr. Telmer told us that the superintendent expects the staff to keep our opinions about all this to ourselves. But that's how I feel. . . . It is."

Jill said, "We've got something to tell you—can the four of us go into the workroom for a few minutes?"

The librarian hesitated, then said, "Does this have something to do with your question about the stars?"

Jill nodded. "Yes, about that, plus a lot more."

Mrs. Sinclair said, "Just let me call Ms. Shubert in the teachers' room so she can cover the front desk. You go in, and I'll be along in a minute."

The three kids moved all their stuff from the alcove into the glass-walled room. They sat at the worktable, and immediately Jill said, "You were right about her, Robert. Completely. And I was wrong."

"No problem," he said. "It was good to be sure. You were right too."

Jill said, "Well, it's sure a good thing that Lyman had to go and fix—" but she stopped when she saw the grin on Ben's face.

"*Ohhh!*" she said slowly, smiling at him. "You clever, *clever* boy! You texted Mrs. Hinman, up on the third floor, and told her we needed a diversion!"

"I *may* have done something like that," he

said. "You're not the only one who knows how to use a secret agent."

Ben was expecting a bit more praise for his remote control rescue mission, but Jill had moved on.

Looking at Robert, she said, "So, what do you think is the best way to have Mrs. Sinclair help?"

Robert shrugged. "That's sort of up to her. We've got to tell her everything we know, get her up to speed, and then see if she has an idea about how to focus in on that one still star."

As the two of them talked, that old feeling of being left out crept into Ben's head, along with some jealousy for Gerritt, for how smart he was. But he stopped it dead in its tracks.

No—this is good! Because my first job is to keep everyone working together.

It was a freeing thought—so freeing that he suddenly felt like he was far above the workroom, even above the school and the whole town, and as he looked down, he could see all the different resources that the Keepers and the Glennley Group were bringing to this fight. It reminded him of the way old-time admirals used to put little models of all their ships onto a huge flat map, then move the models around to trace the progress of the war and to plan the next steps. He could see everything.

And he saw that the entire war now depended on the successful action of just one warship . . . the USS *Oakes*—and he was the captain, Captain Benjamin Pratt . . . or at least, the temporary captain. And the biggest part of his job right now? He had to help the Keepers do their best work, each one of them. And it was up to him to set the example and boost the morale of the whole crew.

Because Captain Pratt knew about warships. Without true and constant teamwork, without smart, unselfish labor, a battle could be lost long before the cannonballs began to fly.

And this battle was already raging. The first shots had been fired, and now it was do-or-die. They were facing a pirate ship . . . the *Glennley Beast*. And each ship was trying to get into a commanding position. The *Beast* was well-armed, its crew was tough, and Captain Lyman was ruthless. And unless the *Oakes* could . . .

"Now, tell me what all this is about."

Mrs. Sinclair sat across the table and her

bright gray eyes looked straight at him. Ben came back to earth very fast—but not completely.

Instead of starting to tell the librarian himself, he said, "Robert, why don't you explain."

Because that was the move Captain Pratt would have made.

CHAPTER 17

Dog on a Chain

Mrs. Sinclair wasn't just interested in what Robert told her about the Keepers—she was thrilled by it, and even more excited when Jill asked her to take the oath of secrecy and join up—which she did.

"I *knew* it!" she said, looking around the workroom table at them. "I just *knew* you three were up to something special! In the twenty-three years I've been here, no research group has *ever* put in the kind of time and effort that you have, and now I see why!"

Ben said, "Well, we've made a lot of progress, but we're not sure if what we've already got is enough to stop Glennley. What we need right now is to keep Lyman and Wally away from that sextant—I don't think Lyman saw it. And we also need to open the case so we can see if the last safeguard is in there."

Mrs. Hinman stood up and said, "Let's go take a look."

Before they even got close to the case, Ben noticed something he'd missed earlier—they all saw it.

Jill said, "There's a keyhole!"

Mrs. Sinclair said, "And I don't have the key—of course, I've never really looked for it. . . ."

Robert pulled up on the front of the case. "Yup, definitely locked."

Ben hurried back to the workroom, fumbled with his backpack, then trotted back and lay the big key ring on the display case in front of Mrs. Sinclair.

The librarian's mouth dropped open. "How in the world . . . ?"

Ben said, "Mr. Keane left these with his wife, and he asked her to give them to me."

Robert pointed: "Try that one."

They all stared: Robert had spotted a small key that featured a distinctive design—a star!

Ben slipped it into the keyhole and twisted. With a soft click, the front edge of the top rose a quarter of an inch. Mrs. Sinclair and Jill took hold and lifted upward until the hinged lid was all the way open.

Robert reached for the sextant box, but Ben said, "Wait a second," and he snapped three pictures. "Okay."

"It's pretty heavy!" Robert set the box on the shelf next to the dictionary. "First off, we should look at the case—see if there's anything else hidden in there."

Mrs. Sinclair immediately picked up the sextant box and said, "I think the first thing to do is to put *this* in a safer place."

She carried it into the workroom, set it on the table, then opened a cabinet and got out a paper tablecloth. She covered the whole thing, and before she came out and shut the door, Ben saw her turn the lock button on the knob.

Rejoining the group, she said, "No one else has a key to that room, so our friendly janitors can now snoop around all they want."

Robert was bent over the display case, tapping the sides and the shelf.

"I'm not seeing any secret hiding places in here—do you guys see anything?"

Ben checked the inside, then lay on the floor and shined his small flashlight up from below.

"Gerritt's right," he said. "There's just that one shelf inside the case, and I can see the underside of the boards. No hidden compartments."

Jill said, "So let's lock it up, put the dictionary back, and check out the sextant."

Mrs. Sinclair handed Jill a key. "You three go and lock yourselves into the workroom. I'll get this area looking normal again and then carry on with my regular work—so no one suspects that I'm part of your team."

The three of them went in and stood around the table, and Jill pulled the cover off the wooden box. Ben started to reach for the sextant, but Robert said, "Hang on, Pratt—let me get some close-up shots with the good camera before we mess with it. From what we know about Old Man Oakes, there could be some kind of message hidden in the way he left the thing set up."

After Gerritt took five or six photos, Ben lifted

the sextant out of the case, and Jill did a careful examination of the box itself, inside and out. She even removed the purple velvet liner. Apart from the inscription on the small brass plaque, there was nothing.

"Heads up!" Gerritt snapped. "Wally!"

Ben tucked the sextant back into its box, and Jill had the whole thing covered again before Wally got close to the workroom. He didn't try to come in, but he definitely wanted to see what they were up to.

He unhooked a spray bottle from a clip on his belt, gave a few quick squirts onto the glass, and then wiped away at it with a cloth—leaving filmy streaks behind. But he wasn't paying attention to anything except the kids, and his small dark eyes instantly focused on the large covered lump on the table.

Robert said, "So it's the old fake-window-washing trick. Two can play that game—watch this."

He pulled a couple of paper towels off a roll, then walked over, stood directly in front of Wally, and began pretending to clean the inside of the glass. He mirrored each of Wally's actions, completely blocking his view. They were almost the same height, and Gerritt smiled right into his face, eye-to-eye.

Jill started to giggle.

As they watched, Wally's face turned a blotchy red, and his lips curled back into an ugly grimace.

Jill stopped giggling. "Um . . . Robert? I don't think it's good to get him *that* mad. . . ."

Robert kept polishing the glass, mimicking Wally's every move.

Speaking softly, he said, "I seem to remember that it was *you* who told us how Stumpy had anger issues—so *I'm* gonna see if he'll blow his top. One big outburst, and he's history—and you have to admit, it would be great to have him disappear."

As usual, it was hard to argue with Gerritt's logic.

But Ben didn't like it. Was this a reaction to what Wally had said to him the other morning? Because what Robert was doing seemed sort of like teasing a dog on a chain—just plain mean.

Wally suddenly turned away and stomped out of the library.

Robert said, "Well, at least I got him to leave."

That was true, but still, it left Ben with a bad feeling.

CHAPTER 18

Aloft

The heat wave, the pressure of finding safeguard number five, the endless hide-and-seek with Lyman and Wally, plus Gerritt's constant sniping and Jill's never-ending touchiness, and Ben was ready to make it official: Tuesday, June 9, was one messed-up day. And it wasn't over—not even close.

Ben wished it was. Except, not really.

But time was almost up. And if he and the other Keepers couldn't solve the final clue and find that last safeguard, that was it. All Glennley had to do was let the clock run out, and it would be game over. So long Oakes School. And Barclay Bay. And Edgeport.

All day long, no matter what kind of emergency Mrs. Hinman or Mrs. Sinclair or any of the other extra Keepers came up with, Lyman or Wally had hovered near Ben and Jill and Robert almost constantly. They were simply ignoring all other requests. For the part of the morning when the three of them had been in the library, one or the other had walked up and down the hall, past the doors, pushing a dust mop.

The one time Ben had managed to sneak away on his own after a trip to the restroom, Mr. Telmer had spotted him in the hallway and ordered him to go outside and join his fourth-period class.

Lunchtime was a waste, because Mrs. Flagg had been instructed not to let any students into the school from the cafeteria for any reason. Everyone had to go back outdoors.

All three of them were going to be at the chorus and orchestra rehearsal after school, but Ben couldn't see that helping much. Even if they could escape Mr. Maasen's watchful eye, it would be a snap for either Lyman or Wally to spot them leaving the auditorium.

And now it was sixth-period gym class, and where were they? Stuck outside, sitting still and sweating.

Lying on the grass beneath an oak, Ben felt like this whole day had been a tragic loss—a wasted opportunity at the worst possible moment. He looked up through the leaves at the hazy sky and saw a lone seagull, floating with the offshore breeze.

Are we really going to be the last kids in the history of Edgeport to finish a school year here?

Ben sat up, opened his iPad, and tapped the screen to access the photos.

Robert had taken some very sharp pictures of the box, the sextant itself, and the small brass plaque. Slowly and carefully, Ben studied each photo and then read the inscription slowly, over and over again. And about the sixth time through the inscription, the last phrase jumped out at him: *Set a true course, and then climb aloft and keep a sharp lookout!*

He pulled a card from his backpack and began scribbling notes.

He nudged Robert. "Hey, Gerritt, remember what you said, about how Captain Oakes used nautical and shipbuilding terms and applied them to the school building?"

Robert didn't stir. "Yeah—upper deck meant third floor, five bells meant six thirty on the chronometer, 'hooks' was short for 'futtocks,' which meant posts in the hallway." He yawned. "So what?"

"So, at the end of the sextant inscription, there are *three* nautical terms in a row—set a true course, climb aloft, and keep a sharp lookout!"

Robert opened one eye. "Are you really just figuring this out, Pratt? Let me translate for you: Find the right direction, then go up to the third floor, and look around carefully. The problem is, Pratt, we've been all over the third floor a million times. We've looked at every door, tried every key in every keyhole, tapped on every wall and the back of every cabinet. And there's *nothing* there. Nothing."

Jill brushed a fly away from her face, but aside from that lay perfectly still on her back, eyes shut. "I know I'm not a supersailor like you two lords of the waves, but isn't 'aloft' different from 'the upper deck'? Like, *higher* than the deck?"

Robert sat straight up. "Jill—that's *brilliant*! Look!"

She rolled over and propped her chin on one elbow. They were at the edge of the field behind the Annex, so they all had a view of the entire back of the original school.

And Jill and Ben saw what Robert was pointing at, clear as day, framed against the blue sky. He was pointing at the cupola, up on the very top of the copper roof.

"That," he said, "is 'aloft'!"

CHAPTER 19

All Worked Out

Mr. Maasen was standing at the main exit of the auditorium, hurrying the kids outdoors. "Remember, you have to be back here at six forty-five to get in place for the concert . . . and don't forget to wear your good clothes . . . and bring your instruments!"

It had been a good rehearsal, but Ben was going nuts. Because the Keepers had a clear objective now. They had to figure out how to "climb aloft" into the cupola so they could find that final safeguard. And they had to do it soon.

But the late bus was waiting at the curb, and

Mr. Maasen was making sure that every single kid exited the building—and *both* janitors had joined him at the doorway.

Jill got to the door before Ben and Robert did, and she stopped and said, "I really need to go get something from my locker."

Mr. Maasen shook his head. "Not possible, Jill. See you at the concert." He pointed out the door.

Wally pointed too. "Yeah," he sneered, "not possible, *Jill*."

Mr. Maasen give the janitor an odd look, and Lyman seemed surprised too. But Wally didn't care, didn't even notice, and Ben got a glimpse of that same anger they'd seen earlier. His face wasn't quite as red as when he had stormed out of the library, but the guy certainly looked strange.

When the three of them had walked around behind the school, Ben almost said, *How about we sneak over to the north side and use Mr. Keane's keys to get in through the door near the library?* But he knew it would be pointless. On his way to the rehearsal, Gerritt had passed the janitor's workroom, and he'd spotted a large cooler by the workbench plus two army-style folding cots leaning against the wall. The Glennley sentries weren't going *anywhere*. Lyman and Wally were going to be patrolling the halls nonstop for the rest of day—and probably all Tuesday night.

So instead, Ben said, "You guys want to come eat dinner over at the boat? We can get pizza and work out a plan for tonight after the concert."

"I've got the plan all worked out," Robert said, "but, sure, pizza sounds good."

Jill glared at Robert, and Ben was glad it wasn't him getting the evil eye.

"All worked out?" she said. "How *nice*. And exactly when were you going to share this great plan of yours—or are we just supposed to wait and enjoy the surprise?"

"Tell you what," Robert said. "You and Pratt walk along with me to my house so I can pick up my clothes for the concert, and on the way I'll explain—which I was going to do anyway. And if you don't like the plan, or if you want to add anything, that'll be great. What I should have said is, 'I've some ideas for tonight.'"

Ben wasn't fooled. Gerritt had meant exactly what he'd said, and on the walk to his grandmother's house, he laid out his plan, step by step. Jill offered a few ideas, but each time, Robert patiently explained why his way was better—and Ben had to agree. The guy really did have it figured out.

The pizza was good, and when they'd eaten, Ben called Tom Benton and asked him to set up a conference call with all the Keepers. And at six o'clock Tuesday evening, everyone was patched in—including the seven new kids, Mrs. Hinman, and Mrs. Sinclair. Ben, Jill, Robert, and Ben's dad sat around one cell phone on the table in the saloon of the *Tempus Fugit*. A light breeze had come up, and the boat bumped gently against the dock, but it didn't make enough noise to bother anyone.

First, Ben brought everyone up to speed on the day's discoveries. He was glad that his dad was sitting there on the couch in their old sailboat, smiling and looking very proud of him. And then a less happy thought: He pictured his mom, sitting alone with her phone at their kitchen table over on Maple Street.

But Ben stayed focused. He couldn't be thinking about personal stuff, not now.

When Ben finished, it was Robert's turn, and he gave a detailed explanation of the plan for the night. When he was done, there were murmurs of agreement and appreciation, and Ben recognized Mrs. Keane's voice saying, "What a marvelous plan!"

But Robert didn't react much to the praise, and when it got quiet, he said, "So . . . are there any ideas about how to make this work better?"

Mrs. Sinclair quickly piped up with a suggestion, and Robert instantly said, "Great—that'll help a lot!"

Which got him a funny look from Jill—Ben saw her eyes narrow, saw her lips press together. Because earlier, Robert had pushed back on every single idea she had offered. But she didn't say anything now.

Then Jill's dad said, "Can someone please tell me why we don't just call all the media outlets, blow the whistle on these two phony janitors, and take over the school and do a huge search for the last safeguard, with all of us in the hunt? How come you kids have to keep sneaking around like this?"

Harold Chamden, the lawyer, spoke up before Robert could reply. "The answer to that is pretty simple. The school superintendent and the school board are eager to have the Glennley deal go through, and so are a lot of the business leaders in the town. And if this turned into a public fight tonight, the superintendent has the authority to cancel the concert, cancel the last half-day of school tomorrow, and demand that the police completely close off the school property—and I think she's capable of doing that. So it's wisest if we wait until tomorrow to launch our legal and public relations blitz."

Mr. Acton wasn't finished. "But couldn't I at least hide somewhere inside the school tonight, just to be there as backup for the kids?"

Ben saw Jill roll her eyes, and then she said into the speakerphone, "Daddy, we've been in there *tons* of times, so stop worrying."

"Those *other* times," he replied, "you were sneaking out in the middle of the night, and I knew nothing about any of this. Now I *know*, and I just don't like the idea of you kids having to deal with those two gorillas on your own."

Again the lawyer replied, "Well, you *could* go and hide in the school, Carl. But if *you* got caught in there? You'd almost certainly be charged with criminal trespass, and probably breaking and entering, too. If the kids got caught, they'd get a scolding—and also, in a worst-case situation, where they had to appear in court? We could introduce Captain Oakes's codicil as evidence that the school actually *belongs* to them and that *their* claim to trusteeship actually precedes the claims of the school board. But again, revealing the codicil now? That would make this fight very public, and if things *don't* go as we hope, then there might never be another opportunity to search for the last safeguard. And, really, I feel quite sure those janitors are not going to do *anything* that might get themselves in trouble with the law—that's the last thing the Glennley side wants." Mr. Chamden cleared his throat, then added, "However, I think it would be an excellent idea to have our own backup in place *outside* the school, but close enough to get there almost instantly if any of the kids call for help. And, Carl, we can work out those details a little later, all right?"

Mr. Acton said, "Yes, that sounds good."

It was quiet for a moment, and then Robert said, "Anything else?"

No one spoke, so Ben said, "Well, it's good there aren't more questions, because we're about out of time—all the kids have to get over to the school soon. So, just remember what you need to do later on, and we'll see everybody at the concert. Thanks a lot. Really, thank you."

A number of voices said, "Good-bye," or "So long," or "Good luck," and then the phone on the table started making noises as all the Keepers disconnected—more than a dozen clicks and beeps.

Those sounds were comforting for Ben—he felt good about their little army. It was a great team. Everyone had a job to do, and if all went according to plan, *this* was going to be quite a night.

CHAPTER 20

Phase One

Ben had a good view from his spot on the back row of the risers, and when the curtain finally opened at seven forty, he watched the principal walk to the center of the stage. The room dimmed, a spotlight focused on Mr. Telmer, and the packed auditorium got quiet.

He looked out over the crowd and then read from the paper in his hand, his voice strong and clear. "'We hold these truths to be self-evident, that all men are created equal, that they are endowed by their Creator with certain unalienable Rights, that among these are Life, Liberty and the pursuit of Happiness.'" He paused, then continued, "When these historic words of our Declaration of Independence were first spoken to the world in 1776, the building that later became the Captain Duncan Oakes School was already standing next to the Atlantic Ocean, right here in Edgeport, Massachusetts." Mr. Telmer paused again and used a knuckle to swipe at the corner of one eye. "Thanks to the dedication and hard work of thousands and thousands of wonderful parents, teachers, and children, this school has stood here like a lighthouse ever since—a beacon of education and freedom. As the current principal and as a fellow citizen, I want to welcome all of you to *this* historic event, this very last concert at our school. The title of the concert is An American Songfest."

Everyone clapped, and as Mr. Telmer walked off the stage, a drum and flute began to play, and the chorus launched into "Yankee Doodle."

Ben didn't think it was weird that the principal had gotten emotional—there were tissues popping out all over the auditorium. Out of the hundreds of people here, all but a handful thought that this was the very last event, the end of an era, the end of the school.

But it's not!

The next sixty minutes zipped by. After

"Yankee Doodle," they sang a sea chantey, and then one of Ben's favorites, "Fifteen Years on the Erie Canal." The song called "Across the Wide Missouri" was from the time when the country was expanding westward, followed by a cowboy song, and then "Casey Jones," a railroad song. About halfway through the concert, they sang "Follow the Drinking Gourd," and then Carolynn Eliot read Lincoln's Gettysburg address. Carolynn was one of the new Keepers, and Ben thought she did a good job. The address was followed by a happy song from that era called "Wait for the Wagon." After a First World War song, "As the Caissons Go Rolling Along," there was a verse from a song about the end of the Great Depression called "Happy Days Are Here Again." Then, while slides showed pictures from the Second World War, Korea, Vietnam, and the most recent wars, they sang "From the Halls of Montezuma"—immediately followed by "Where Have All the Flowers Gone," which was a sad song about dead soldiers.

Even though it was the same music the chorus had practiced over and over for the past month and a half, this time it was different, and Ben got choked up a couple of times. As the concert ended with everyone on their feet for "The Star Spangled Banner," he could barely sing.

But Ben made himself stop feeling and start thinking again. Because tonight's *main* event was just getting started, and these fifteen minutes after the concert were a critical part of Gerritt's plan—Phase One.

When the final applause died down, Ben checked his phone—it was eight forty-two—which meant that he had *exactly* eight minutes to get out into the main lobby and become part of the crowd of kids and parents who would be moving toward the parking lot. Because Gerritt's plan depended on precise timing.

He made his way up the aisle and met up with his mom and dad at the place they had all agreed on, right in front of the big trophy case—which was now empty, since all the cups and plaques and little statues had been moved to the new school. And he spotted Jill as she found her parents, and then he saw Gerritt joining his grandmother.

So far, so good.

He scanned the area for Lyman and Wally.

As Robert had predicted, both men were standing near the main doors that led to the parking lot. Ben was trying to look around casually, but Lyman wasn't. He didn't try to hide the fact that he was closely watching all three kids, and when Ben glanced his way, their eyes met. Lyman smiled slightly and nodded, and Ben quickly looked away—but not before he had a sudden flash of memory. It was that thing Mr. Keane had said to him the morning he died: *Lyman's a snake!*

All that seemed like a million years ago.

Still, a cold, creepy feeling tried to take hold of him, but Ben fought it off.

I am not *the scared little kid I was back then!*

With the sharp precision of a military commander, Ben continued his survey of the area.

Mrs. Keane? *Check*—there inside the doorway, just behind Wally, acting like she was looking outside and waiting for her ride.

Tom Benton? *Check*—standing near the wall on the other side of the doorway, close to Lyman. Tom hadn't been using his walker as much recently, but he'd brought it tonight—because Gerritt had told him to. For a reason.

Ben looked to his left as he and his mom and dad neared the doorway. He was trying to spot one last key player . . . and there he was.

Check.

Mr. Chamden, the lawyer, was about twenty feet behind him and his parents.

Ben saw Gerritt and his grandmother go between Wally and Lyman, then walk outside, and he saw Lyman notice them leave.

Jill and her mom and dad were next through the wide double doors, and again, both Lyman and Wally took note that she was outside now, headed over into the parking lot.

Ben was the last of the three kids to go through the doors, and when he and his parents were outside on the driveway, his mom leaned toward him and whispered, "I don't see why Robert's plan couldn't have included me stopping right there in the doorway and giving Mr. Lyman a black eye!"

Ben smiled, but he whispered, "*Shhh!* Listen for the signal!"

Because he and Jill and Robert were all out among the cars in the parking lot now. It was eight fifty-three. The school's outside floodlights were on, but Ben and Jill and Robert were out where the shadows of the surrounding trees made it much darker.

Taking a quick peek back over his shoulder,

Ben saw that another one of Robert's predictions was correct: Lyman and Wally had moved.

They were standing outside next to the doors now, still watching. Which was *exactly* what Gerritt had said they would do: *So, after the concert, the Two Musketeers are going to keep on watching their three problem children walk away from the school, to make sure that we have truly left for home.*

Any second now, Ben thought, any second . . .

"Ohhhhh!"

It wasn't a scream, but the sound pierced the night.

Mrs. Keane had a strong voice, and all the kids and parents in the parking lot stopped and looked back toward the school.

"This woman needs help, right NOW! You there, go get her a chair!"

That voice was even stronger, a loud, manly voice.

Ben smiled—Tom Benton was acting a little like a crazy man, just like Gerritt had asked him to, towering above Wally, blocking the doorway with his walker, one arm up and pointing at Mrs. Keane. And Wally rushed inside, instantly obeying Tom's command.

And now it was Harold Chamden's move.

He was tall—as tall as Lyman—and he got right up into the janitor's face, pointing at Mrs. Keane, talking fast and demanding Lyman's full attention for about ten seconds.

And then, Mrs. Hinman, who was also fairly tall, took up her position, pretending to look at Mrs. Keane, but standing so that she completely blocked Lyman's view of the school parking lot . . . for about ten seconds.

And ten seconds was enough.

The crisis ended quickly, and the instant Mr. Chamden and Mrs. Hinman moved on, Lyman quickly peered back toward the darkened parking lot. And what Lyman saw was just exactly what Lyman wanted to see, what he *needed* to see: Because there was Ben, walking away between his mom and dad . . . and there was Jill, leaving with her parents . . . and there was Robert, headed home with his grandmother, still holding on to her arm.

That's how it looked.

But it was Gabe Dalton walking with Mr. and Mrs. Pratt, and it was Jennie Arling there between Mr. and Mrs. Acton, and the tall young man holding

on to Robert's grandmother's arm? That was Joey Slade, another of the new Keepers that Ben had recruited during social studies yesterday afternoon.

Three minutes later one more of Gerritt's predictions came true, because when Ben tried to put the key into the lock on the door on the north side of the school, it wouldn't go in, and a quick check with a small flashlight showed why: Lyman or Wally had filled up the keyhole with some kind of hard white glue.

But it didn't matter. Because thirty seconds later, at *exactly* eight fifty-eight, Mrs. Sinclair pushed the door open from the inside and whispered, "Phase One, complete!"

CHAPTER 21

The Waiting

Ben was wide awake. He looked at his phone for the sixth time—only eleven forty-five. He was supposed to be napping, but he just couldn't get comfortable. Or shut off his thinker.

He heard low, regular breathing from underneath the table along the other wall of the library workroom—Gerritt wasn't snoring, but he was definitely asleep. And just a foot away, by the dim light of his phone, he could see Jill's face—calm, completely composed, a slight smile on her lips, out cold. The phone winked off, but the image of her face was still there, lit up in his mind. A good face.

When Mrs. Sinclair had let them into the school and then led them to the library, Ben had pointed at a painting on the hallway wall and whispered, "What happened there?"

It was a large painting, almost three feet wide, and it was one of Ben's favorites—a winter scene of Edgeport Harbor, painted in 1822. But now the entire thing was covered with a white plastic wrap.

Mrs. Sinclair didn't slow down, didn't answer until she'd unlocked the darkened library and let them inside. When the door was shut behind them, she spoke softly. "That painting? A group from the town manager's office came through, and all the paintings and everything else that's hanging on the walls of the school has been wrapped and labeled—some things will go to the library, some to the historical society, some to the new school, and a few are going to the Peabody Essex Museum. They'll all be taken away tomorrow after school, before the salvage crew comes in to remove the doors and the cabinets, all the old hardware and fixtures—anything that can be sold or reused. Before the demolition starts."

Her answer had shocked him, and as Mrs. Sinclair opened the workroom and showed them where they'd be hiding out, Ben had had trouble paying attention. Because there were all these people—dozens, maybe hundreds of serious, careful people—who were already starting to treat the school like it was dead. It reminded him of a nature program he'd seen, where a fallen zebra got torn to pieces and carried off in different directions by lions and hyenas and jackals.

And now, lying on the carpeted floor underneath a table, hidden behind cardboard packing boxes and stacks of books, with Jill and Robert sound asleep nearby, that image of the zebra came to haunt him again. He couldn't remember a moment when he'd felt more uncertain, or more alone.

No . . . that wasn't quite true. The afternoon when his mom and dad had told him they were going be separated? That was worse. But this was a close second. He hated thinking about that huge pack of predators, circling around the school, nipping, biting, getting ready to rush in for the kill. Ben shivered at the thought.

I can't just lie here, not until two a.m.—no way!

Because that was Gerritt's plan—get inside, hide in a safe place, lay low until Lyman and Wally were asleep, and then sneak up to the third floor and figure out how to "climb aloft."

Ben turned carefully onto his back and lit up his phone again. All the pictures he'd been looking at this afternoon on his iPad were also on the phone—the complete photographic record of their hunt for the safeguards. The pictures were hard to see on the little screen. Jill's mom had brought their backpacks and given them to Mrs. Sinclair before the concert, and his was under the table, down near his feet. So his iPad was close. But turning onto his back had made Jill stir, and he didn't want to risk disturbing her rest just so he could have a bigger screen to look at.

He scrolled through all the pictures, one by one, not fast, not slow, just letting his mind roll along with the flow of the past twenty-six days. And where there were gaps in the pictures, his mind filled in the other events—like the day after school when that sleazy real estate lawyer had come to talk to his mom . . . or when he'd sailed down to Duxbury and back with his dad over Memorial Day weekend. So much had happened.

He had some great pictures of Jill. Robert too; lots of good shots of Gerritt. But the pictures he looked at the longest were the ones of Jill—until he noticed that was what he was doing.

When he got to the last of the pictures, the ones he'd taken today, Ben checked the time again—eleven fifty-eight, not even midnight. Two more hours.

Ben pulled in a deep breath, then let it out slowly.

He clicked on the first photograph and began again, scrolling through the pictures. This time, he forced himself to slow down, made himself look carefully at every picture, made himself think.

If I go slowly enough, it might eat up a whole half hour. . . . It might even put me to sleep.

Of the first twenty pictures or so, about half of them were shots of the pages of the big book about the building of the school, the one with the great drawings the carpenter had made. Except on the phone screen, all of John Vining's drawings were ridiculously small.

This is nuts. . . . The book itself is only thirty feet away . . . and getting over there without waking anyone up? That would be a worthy test of my ninja skills!

Except . . . what if Lyman or Wally walked past on patrol?

Nah—not gonna happen. And anyway, it's so quiet, I'd hear them and have plenty of time to hide. Plus, I'll be out and back in less than ten minutes!

Before he moved a muscle, before he even decided to actually give it a try, Ben pictured each motion, each step, every inch he'd need to travel. And then he began.

Turning very slowly onto his left side, he reached out with one hand and pushed against the large box Mrs. Hinman had placed in front of the table he and Jill were under. The cardboard sliding on the carpet made a loud hiss, so he stopped, let the silence settle, and began again, this time barely moving the box.

After he'd shifted the box about eighteen inches, he began to move himself, slowly rolling over onto his stomach. Then it was like doing a slow-motion push-up, until he was on his hands and knees, inching backward out from under the table. After a few minutes, he was clear of the box and the table, so he stood up, reached down, and slowly slid the cardboard box back where it had been. Then he tiptoed over to the workroom door.

The door was a problem—knobs and latches often made sharp, mechanical clicks, which would almost certainly wake Robert or Jill. But he got a good grip on the doorknob, pushed gently on the door, and at the same time turned the knob ever so slowly. The door opened noiselessly.

Jill had given him Mrs. Sinclair's key to the workroom, so he was able to shut the door from the outside, slowly let the knob turn back into place, and set the latch. Then he eased the key into the lock, turned it to the left, turned it back to the upright position, and then gently removed it. All locked up again.

The red glow of the exit light let him see where he was going, and the lamps along the harbor walk cast a glimmer through the windows that faced east. But he could have found his way to the reference area in complete darkness. That's where he and Jill had had their first big confrontation with Lyman—when she had stared right into the guy's face and told him that he was unpleasant to look at, and that, yes, he had this deep, creepy voice, but that he wasn't scaring her one bit! The memory made him grin into the darkness. That girl had *guts*!

Ben was glad to see that the old book hadn't been packed away yet, but it did have a yellow tag on its spine—its new home was going to be in the town library. He pulled it slowly off the shelf, went to the north wall of the room, and settled on the floor behind a tall bookcase. He lit up his phone. It wasn't a great reading light, but it was all he had, and as he opened the book he also checked the time on the screen: only twelve seventeen. He started to groan, but stopped and scolded himself.

Yeah, two o'clock is still a long way off, but so what? When would I ever get this much time to actually read a great old book? So shut up and enjoy it!

He began at the beginning, with the foreword—which he never did. The foreword of a book always seemed like a nuisance, something to skip past on the way to the *real* beginning.

But this foreword? It was about the story *before* the story of the school. Duncan's father, Samuel Oakes, had come to the Massachusetts Bay Colony in 1681, married, and he and his wife had six children. But only three survived beyond childhood, two boys and a girl.

Duncan was their youngest son, and he was

remarkably intelligent. At age sixteen, he was sent to Harvard University to study to become a minister, but after graduating, he chose to become a merchant, and then a trader, sailing a very small boat up and down the coast of New England.

When Ben turned the page, there was a fine black-and-white print of that great life-size portrait of Captain Oakes, the one that was hanging on the wall up in the third-floor hallway.

Ben angled the light from his cell phone so he could get a better look at the captain's face. He had a strong, squared-off chin, a high forehead, and his eyes seemed to be looking far off into the distance—and what he was seeing brought a small, satisfied smile to his lips. And, of course, the captain was standing on the quarterdeck of a ship, in full uniform. Aiming the phone so it lit up the whole picture, Ben noticed that the captain held something in his right hand—maybe a chart? It wasn't a very clear print. And there was something else in his left hand, mostly hidden—

Oh—it's a dagger . . . no, more like a pistol . . . or a boarding axe . . .

Several things happened almost at the same

moment. Because as Ben saw something remarkable right there in the book—so remarkable that he gasped—at that *exact* instant he heard loud voices, the library door burst open, and someone turned on all the lights.

CHAPTER 22

The Last Word

Ben was as far from the main door as it was possible to be, without diving out a window on the north wall—which is what he wished he could do. Because if Lyman or Wally were to take a simple stroll around the library, there was no way he could hide.

But they walked straight toward the workroom. And they were arguing, too, almost yelling at each other.

"I don't care one bit what you *think* you've been told to do!" Lyman shouted. "Because I *know* what I've been told to do, and *I'm* the one who's still in charge here. You got it?"

"Yeah, I *got* it," Wally snapped. "What I've *got* is that *you* think you're the big cheese, just like always, and I'm sick of it. And if you hadn't interfered with *my* plans for the flood, we'd be anchored in Kingston harbor right now, sipping our drinks. But no, you had to have it your way, and you messed up! And everyone *knows* you messed up, because *I* told them so, all the higher-ups at headquarters. They all know what a joke you've made of this whole thing, letting a pack of little creeps run circles around you!"

Both men were standing next to the glass-walled workroom now, and Ben had a sudden panic attack. Had he moved anything other than that box when he'd snuck out of there? And was that box back in its right place? He was almost certain everything was okay—almost. . . .

Because the stacks of books and the cardboard boxes had been arranged very carefully in case this very thing happened—so that if the janitors came in and looked around, the kids hiding under the tables would be completely hidden from view.

Jill! What's she going through right now?

Ben imagined her waking from a deep sleep to the sound of those men arguing, with all the lights blazing—and then to realize that *he* was missing!

Crouched near the floor behind the bookcase, Ben peeked between the stacks. The lights in the workroom were off, so Lyman had a high-powered flashlight aimed at the lump hidden under the tablecloth on the center table—the sextant box. The light almost made the thin paper disappear, but not quite. There was still no way to tell what was under there.

"All right, all right," Lyman said, waving one hand dramatically. "*You're* the big genius, and I'm the goat. But I know for *sure* that the kids you're calling 'little creeps'—who are all at least six times smarter than *you* or *I* will ever be—they were excited about

195

that thing this morning, and somehow they got the librarian to lock it up for them. So go ahead, Mr. Genius. You were bragging to me about your successful life as a master criminal and how you learned to pick any lock on earth, right? So here's your big chance: Pick *this* one!"

Ben saw Wally pull a small packet from his shirt pocket, and then bend low over the doorknob. From thirty feet away Ben heard little metallic clicks and scratchings, and several times he heard Wally muttering and swearing under his breath.

And he saw Lyman, leaning against the glass wall beside the door, clearly enjoying himself as Wally got more and more frustrated.

Abruptly, Wally straightened up and banged both fists against the door. The whole room shook, and Ben cringed, imagining how Jill must have jumped at that noise. And Robert, too.

"Why are we even messing around with this stuff?" Wally fumed. "I'm just gonna go grab a pipe wrench and twist that doorknob clean off!"

"No, we're *not* doing that," said Lyman with quiet authority. "That's *exactly* what everyone is waiting for, a chance to catch us damaging the place before the school year is up—which would violate the terms of the agreement, which could provide grounds for a delay, or fines, or even a breach-of-contract dispute. And for all we know, that's the whole point of this little secret treasure they've got on display there—to get *us* to do something stupid. So let's go, okay?"

Ben was surprised to hear how Lyman's tone of voice had changed.

"Look, Wally, I'm doing my best here. And I'm sorry if it seems like I'm tough on you. But I kid you not, I am just as tough on myself, probably even tougher. So let's go get a cold drink, and calm down, and get some rest. In less than twenty-four hours, the deal will be settled, and then we'll get on a plane, go catch up with my boat in Maryland, and spend a month in Jamaica. Does that sound good?"

Ben was puzzled—it sounded like Lyman was talking to a little kid, not a grown-up. . . . Then he got it! Lyman was worried—worried that Wally was cracking up! He was trying to keep a lid on things just long enough to get the job done.

Wally smiled a little. "Yeah, it *does* sound good. But I'd still love to take a hammer to that door, just for the fun of it!"

"I tell you what," said Lyman, putting an arm across Wally's shoulders as they walked toward the exit. "I'll talk to the demolition foreman and see if he'll let you have first swing at the front doors of the school—go at 'em with a twelve-pound sledge hammer! How would that be, huh?"

"Sweet!" said Wally. "But I just hope I get to see the look on the face of that smart-mouthed little girl when I bust 'em down!"

The lights went off, the door was closed and locked, and Ben heard the men talking as they walked along the hallway, headed around to the janitor's room.

Ben didn't think it was a good idea to just rush over and tap on the door of the workroom, not immediately. So he crept to the reference section and put the book away.

He thought he could hear Jill and Robert whispering, so he worked up his courage and went to the door. He got out the key, but then stopped. Because he knew he was going to get yelled at by both of them—or at least whispered at.

He didn't stick to the plan.

He could have been caught.

He could have ruined the whole night, could have completely trashed their last chance to find the final safeguard.

All true.

Then Ben smiled. He walked back to the reference section, slid the big book off the shelf again, and carried it to the workroom.

He whispered at the door, "Hey, it's me—open up."

Because after Jill grouched at him, after Robert informed him what an idiot he was, Ben knew that *he* was going to have the last word. He had news—*big* news.

Because in that picture the painting up on the third floor? Just as Wally and Lyman had arrived, he had realized what Captain Oakes was holding in his left hand.

It was a sextant.

CHAPTER 23

Art Meets Life

Even after hearing Ben's big news, Robert was still furious, and even in whispers, his anger came through loud and clear.

"What's the use of even *having* a plan if you're not going to follow it? It's no good, Pratt, it's no good!"

Ben hissed right back. "So you're saying it would be better if I had just stayed under the table, slowly going crazy, instead of following up on a good idea—*and* finding an important clue? All for the sake of your perfect little plan?

Is that what you're saying? Really? *Really?*"

Jill was fed up. "Quit it, both of you! It's possible, you know, that two people can be right about a different view of the exact same thing, and *this* is one of those things. So just let it go, *both* of you!"

The next hour and a half felt like an eternity to Ben, but neither he nor Jill had the nerve to suggest a change to the timing Robert had worked out. But finally it was two o'clock, and Gerritt whispered, "Okay, let's go."

The trip up the north stairwell was smooth and silent, apart from the occasional creaky step. All three of them went very slowly, keeping their footsteps as close as possible to the wall. And each noise was heard only once, because Jill and Robert avoided the squeaks that Ben discovered.

Ben breathed a little easier when they stepped out into the third-floor hallway. The janitor's room was on the west side of the school, exactly opposite from their destination—the tall portrait of Captain Oakes, which was less than halfway along the east corridor.

What he hadn't counted on was the heavy white plastic that completely covered the painting now—it had been tagged, intended for the new school over on the west side of Route 128. Up close, Ben saw that it was industrial-strength shrink-wrap—the same kind used to cover boats for the winter.

"Here," Robert said, "I'll deal with that."

Ben smiled, because apparently, Gerritt truly *had* planned for everything. He opened the blade of a tiny Swiss Army knife and neatly slit the plastic near the wall on the right side, starting as high as he could reach and continuing down to the bottom corner of the frame.

"Okay, Pratt," he said, handing Ben the knife, "I'll boost you up—slit along the whole top and then down the edge to where I started."

Ben followed instructions, and when he finished, the covering peeled away and dropped softly to the floor.

All three of them stood back, and Jill had her headlamp on now.

Ben had passed this painting several times a day for his whole sixth-grade year, but he felt like he was really *seeing* it for the first time. The black-and-white print in the old book had come nowhere close to capturing its spirit—there was so much life and action up there on the wall.

First of all, he could see there was a brisk breeze blowing—twelve to fifteen knots, judging by the size of the seas off beyond the rail of the ship, and also judging by the angle of the deck below the captain's feet. In the bright midday light, he saw that slight wisps of spray had left beads of moisture on the black leather of the captain's boots. But just as Ben had noticed in that reproduction in the book, it was the captain's face and especially his eyes that were the focal point of the whole painting.

Looking at the book earlier, Ben had guessed correctly—it was a nautical chart that Captain Oakes held in his right hand. But close up like this, he recognized the shoreline. It was Edgeport, and on the map there was a mark, precisely where the school was located—it was the same chart he had seen lying on that map table in the underground room!

And there, now clearly visible, was a full-size image of the same brass sextant that lay downstairs in the library—or rather, the half of the instrument that wasn't hidden behind the captain's left leg.

"Okay, guys," Gerritt said, "there has to be

a reason that the captain brought us here. Let's figure this out."

Jill was already up next to the painting, looking at the heavy carved picture frame, the bright beam of her headlamp aimed just inches before her eyes. Ben was doing the same thing on the other side, carefully inspecting the frame and where it met the wall. He pulled gently outward on the thick edge of the carved wood—no give at all. The frame was a good four inches wide, and it was fastened directly to the wall—he could see the screw heads. Through the years, the workers adding fresh coats of paint to the walls had run their brushes right against the frame—and there were no breaks, no cracks. Anyone trying to remove this painting would need a hammer and a chisel to work it loose.

Robert gently pushed on the canvas itself, then tapped on it.

"Listen," he whispered, and he tapped again on the canvas. There was a wooden sound.

Jill said, "I think that's normal. With a painting this big, there would have to be a layer of wooden boards behind the canvas, to help keep the frame together. That's what we're hearing."

Then Jill gave a soft gasp. "Check this out!" And she pointed at the center of the bottom edge of the frame.

Ben leaned in close, and in the bright LED light he saw a small brass plate screwed to the frame and fancy lettering on it—the title of the painting.

"One Still Star"
by John Singleton Copley

"Cool!" Gerritt whispered. Then he said, "But . . . we're still not *getting* it—what are we supposed to *do* with this information?"

Jill stepped to the far side of the hall, then she whispered, "Hey, get out of the way so I can see the whole thing. . . . Good." Speaking slowly, she said, "Okay . . . we know how the captain keeps comparing this building to a ship." She paused a moment, then said, "So . . . what part of his ship am I looking at there, in the painting?"

With no hesitation Ben said, "That's the quarterdeck, which is sort of the captain's private walking space on deck, near the ship's wheel and the compass binnacle. And see those two small windows and that door there to his left? That's the captain's cabin."

Jill squinted at the painting. Then she shrugged off her backpack, unzipped the main compartment, and dug around for a few seconds.

Ben saw her pull out the large iron key that they had discovered just a few feet from where he was standing, hidden behind a piece of wooden floor molding—the key that was inscribed with a warning: USE ONLY IF YOU MUST.

"What are you doing?" he whispered.

"Thinking," she said. "And looking."

She stepped closer to the painting, and the beam from her headlamp narrowed. And Ben saw what she was looking at: the painted door of the captain's cabin. She moved closer still, until the beam was about as big around as a basketball, then a softball, and finally a tennis ball. And now Ben saw what she was seeing, and so did Robert. Because that painted door also had a painted keyhole.

Jill lifted the iron key, and before either he or Gerritt could say a word, she pressed the end of it right against the brittle canvas.

"Hey!" Ben said. "That'll rip th—"

But the key *didn't* rip the canvas.

Instead, a small piece flipped up out of the way—a flap of canvas that must have been glued to the back of the painting. And Jill pushed the big key straight into the painted keyhole of the painted door.

She looked at Robert and Ben, her headlamp beam lighting one face, then the other. She whispered, "The key's in as far as it'll go—what should I do?"

Instantly, Ben said, "Turn it!"

Robert added, "Yeah . . . try turning clockwise!"

With both hands on the large round end of the key, Jill applied a steady pressure.

In the silent hallway, the sound of metal rubbing against metal seemed loud, and when Jill had completed a half turn of the key, there was a definite *click*, and an even louder scraping sound—but not metallic.

The frame of the painting, the part that was fastened to the wall, stayed put. But halfway across the width of the wooden frame, a vertical crack opened up, and the whole right edge of the painting moved outward a quarter of an inch.

"Pull," Gerritt whispered. "Pull on the key!"

Jill did, and Ben could see that she didn't have to pull very hard. And when she did, the whole painting creaked and swung toward her, like a door.

The entire back side of the painting was exactly that—a door, a six-paneled pine door, complete with a tarnished brass knob and a boxy-looking surface-mounted lock, the lock Jill had just opened!

"Wow—look at *that*!" Ben said breathlessly.

They looked upward into the darkness, all three of them.

What they saw was a staircase, steep and narrow.

And all three of them knew *exactly* what they were going to do next.

CHAPTER 24

Cleared for Action

Jill led the way, and the steps they climbed weren't like a staircase at all. Ben realized it was more like a ladder up a narrow passageway on board a ship, complete with a narrow grip rail along each side.

He was counting, and when he had climbed twenty-two steps, Jill whispered, "Stop! There are boards above my head!"

Ben said, "It's probably a hatch cover—push up on the front edge, the part closest to the steps."

He was right. The hinged lid was less than two feet square, and it opened near the center of the room. Once they had all clambered up, Robert closed it.

The inside of the cupola reminded Ben of the secret room in the sub-basement, the one hidden behind the tide mill—except this room seemed smaller than he had expected. He had looked up at the cupola for as long as he could remember, a little house perched on the school's roof, and he had imagined lots of space, and being able to walk around and look out all the windows.

But standing inside it now, there was no nighttime view of the shoreline and the bay—no view at all. The room was completely closed in. So those outer windows were only for show, which was kind of a sad discovery.

But it made sense to Ben. There must have been some other access to the *outside* of the cupola, maybe a walkway across the roof. Because over the last two centuries, workers would have certainly climbed up to check the roof for leaks, and the wooden window frames would have needed fresh paint every ten or fifteen years. But the inner room had remained untouched.

Like that hidden basement room, this one had also been lined with copper sheeting to make a completely weather-tight box. Ben had thought it would be boiling hot up here, the way his attic room at home sometimes got during a heat wave. But there must have been some kind of ventilation system or thick insulation, because it was surprisingly cool—much cooler than the third-floor hallway had been.

There was a sudden squeak, very close, and they all froze.

Then came another one, and Gerritt smiled, pointing upward.

"Relax," he whispered, "it's the weather vane turning, up on top."

A secret door behind a painting, a climb up thirty-three steps, a room with no windows and completely lined with copper—all very strange. But the oddest thing of all? The room was empty, completely bare. No furniture, no chests, nothing.

Ben could tell that Jill and Robert had felt the same stab of disappointment.

Gerritt was the first to say it.

"So," he began slowly, "looks a *lot* like a dead end."

"C'mon, guys," Ben said. "There *has* to be something here, something that's not obvious.

Maybe there was even something we missed on the way up the ladder."

"Or," Gerritt said, "maybe Lyman and his gang got up in here three weeks ago and they carted off whatever *used* to be here, and now we're sitting here like a bunch of chumps. How about *that*, Pratt? Because *this* is an empty room."

It was that tone again, that same, superior, sarcastic tone. Ben really hated it, and he wanted to rush right over to Gerritt, shove him down backward onto the floorboards, and land one good punch, right on his freckled nose—it would just feel so *good*!

But for the thousandth time in the past month, Ben forced himself to stop feeling and keep thinking.

He took a deep breath and let it out slowly.

"Look, we all worked really hard to get here, and as bad as it *looks*, we *have* to study every square inch of this whole room. So, let's turn our headlamps up as bright as they'll go and give it another fifteen minutes, or as long as it takes. But we *have* to do this—we have to. So, Gerritt, you take that end, I'll take this end of the room, and Jill, you take the middle section.

Walls, floor, ceiling, let's look at *everything—* okay?"

Ben didn't wait for either of them to reply, but simply began the work at his end of the space, the south side of the room. And he was relieved to see that Jill and Robert followed his lead.

The walls at his end of the room were not hiding any mysteries. The edges of all the copper sheets had been sealed with melted lead, and there were no cracks, no open seams, no places where there could be a hidden doorway or a secret compartment. And the ceiling was the same way.

The floorboards were heavy oak, and each plank was nailed into place with large nails, their rounded heads sticking up slightly above the surface. A few of the boards squeaked underfoot, but Ben didn't think there was anything unusual about that. Still, he wanted to be completely thorough, so he got on his hands and knees and inched back and forth across the room, following each plank from wall to wall, looking for something, anything.

He was on his fifth board when Jill whispered, "Um . . . Ben? You need to see this—you too, Robert."

Jill had raised the hatch, and she was leaning forward into the staircase, her head actually down below the level of the floor, aiming her phone camera at something. As Ben and Robert walked over, she snapped a picture with the flash on and then straightened up. She tapped on the screen, adjusted the size, then aimed it at them.

"Check it out!"

Ben squinted. Right on the end of the plank in the center of the hatchway, there was a tiny indentation in the wood.

It was Gerritt who said it out loud. "That's *definitely* a star! But . . . why?"

Ben backed down the ladder into the passageway until he stood at eye level with the ends of the planks, his headlamp aimed straight ahead.

"The center plank, the one with the star? See the edges on both sides, how they run straight up and down? Now look at the next planks, the ones out on either side. Look at how the edges are different. Those are called tongue-and-groove planks, so the boards are joined together tightly along their entire edges. But this center plank? It's *not* tongue-and-groove—get it? So the center board can be pulled straight up!"

Ben stepped down another rung on the ladder and put his hand under the edge of the board with the star on it. "Okay, you guys get shoulder to shoulder on your knees on either side of this board in the middle, but keep off of it. And then both of you get one hand around the end of the board, and when I count to three, I'll push, and both of you pull up. One, two . . ."

"Pratt, you're nuts!" whispered Gerritt. He pointed at the top of the plank. "Look at the size of those nails—they're practically spikes! We're gonna need a crowbar and a hammer to even *start* to get this board out!"

Ben glared at him. "Just give it a try, okay, Gerritt? On three . . . ready? One, two, *three*!"

The board practically flew upward, and Jill and Robert had jump to keep it from clattering onto the floor—which would have woken up Lyman and Wally for sure.

Ben almost said, *See, it wasn't a stupid idea, Gerritt, you grumpy, sarcastic* idiot!

But he didn't.

And then Gerritt surprised him.

"Wow," he said. "I was completely wrong!

Look, all the nails are fake! None of them go through the board!"

Jill said, "So . . . this is a false floor?"

Ben said, "We'll know in second."

He climbed up out of the staircase, but left the hatch up. "Here, grab the edge of the next board, this one on the left. But it's part of that tongue-and-groove system, so instead of pulling *up*, we need to pull it loose first, straight toward the right. On three . . . one, two, three."

The plank groaned a little as its grooved edge separated from the next board, but it came free.

"Look," Gerritt said, "same deal—fake nails!"

Jill ripped off her headlamp and lay on her stomach, peering below the other planks. "This is it, guys, this is it! There's stuff down there . . . chests or something! And one of them is *huge*!"

In less than ten minutes, twenty-one planks had been removed and quietly stacked against the north and south walls of the room. The copper-clad walls extended downward, about three and half feet below the level of the old floor, and met the new floor—which was also covered with copper, just like the floor of the secret room in the basement.

One long supporting beam ran lengthwise

through the center of the space—the board that had held up the planks of the false floor, but Ben saw that it was cut in two. After the three of them lifted off each half-beam and then the chunky center support, the space was open and clear— except for the things Jill had seen.

Three low tables stood directly opposite the stairway hatch, two of them smaller, and a really large one in the center—six or seven feet long. Actually, Ben was only guessing they were tables. He could see what looked like table legs, but each object was covered almost to the floor with heavy canvas—and with a layer of dust that hadn't been disturbed for centuries.

Pointing to the left, Ben said, "Should we look at that one first?"

"Sure," said Gerritt.

"Wait," Jill whispered. "Look!"

Ben got closer with his headlamp, and Robert snapped a quick photo.

In front of the thing on the right, the numeral *1* had been stamped neatly into the copper on the floor. A quick inspection showed the item on the left was labeled *2,* and the large object in the center was marked *3.*

"So," Gerritt said, "now we know. Old Man Oakes is still calling the shots. Hang on a second while I switch the camera to video. . . . Okay, Pratt, let's see what's behind curtain number one."

Ben lifted the cover off—it was a glass top display case, almost identical to the one in the library where they had found the sextant, except this one didn't have a lock. But the hinged top had been sealed shut with pitch—the same sealing method Ben had now seen twice before, complete with an embedded wire for opening it. Jill and Robert crowded in beside him, bending over to look through the glass.

From behind the camera, Gerritt said, "That looks like silk wrapping—open it up!"

Ben ripped the wire free all the way around the edge of the lid, and bits of brittle pitch flew off in every direction. Then he and Jill lifted the front edge of the heavy lid and leaned it against the wall behind the case.

Robert got between them, aiming the camera right down into the case. It was like he was directing a movie.

"Now, both of you reach in from the sides

and unfold the edges of the silk. . . . And keep your heads back so I get a clear shot."

They unfolded the cloth side-to-side first, and then peeled a layer frontward, and folded the final layer toward the back.

"Holy moly!" said Ben.

Gerritt whispered, "Is that . . . ?"

Jill said, "Yes—the Declaration of Independence!"

Then she asked, "But . . . like, it's a *copy*, right?"

"Yeah, of course," said Ben, "but it's still *amazing*!" He knew exactly what he was looking at. "This is called the Dunlap broadsheet, and these were the very first official printed copies— incredibly rare!"

Jill gave him squinty look. "And . . . you know this *how*?"

"'Cause my grandfather took me to the Maine Historical Society on a rainy day last summer, and I studied an identical copy there. And one *just* like this sold for *eight million bucks* about ten years ago! And see the bottom there, the handwriting and the signature? *Nobody's* got a copy like this one!"

Across the bottom of the paper were the

words, "For Duncan Oakes, a true Patriot," and then an unmistakable signature:

"So, do you think the signature and all would make it worth, like, fifteen million?"

Ben grinned. "Who knows? Stuff like this is . . . it's just priceless! And there's *tons* more! Well . . . three or four, anyway."

As gently as possible, he lifted the edge of the heavy paper.

The other documents were just as amazing, each separated by a single sheet of fine white silk. There was Captain Oakes's commission as a naval officer—a handwritten parchment signed by members of the first congress; a personal letter from George Washington thanking him for his military service; another letter signed by John Paul Jones; a printed copy of the US Constitution dated 1789—this one with a personal note signed by John Adams; and also from 1789, a printing of an early draft of the Bill of Rights.

Ben whispered a breathless description of each item for Robert's video. With these things alone, someone could set up a fabulous museum! Still he could tell that he was more excited about these things than Jill or Robert was.

"Okay," said Gerritt, when he'd reached the bottom of the stack. "Let's get to the next one, Pratt."

But Ben wouldn't be hurried. He carefully restacked the documents, putting the sheets of silk between them, then folded the outer covering so the collection was just as they'd found it.

"And now, secret number two," Gerritt said, moving to the left side. "Jill, how about you lift the cover this time?"

Jill removed the dusty cloth, and it was another display case, slightly larger, but in every other way identical to the first, and sealed the same way.

Getting in for a close-up with the camera, Robert said, "That is *beautiful!*"

There was just one thing in the case: a perfect scale model of a twenty-four-gun frigate. The gun ports on both sides of the ship stood open, and it was fitted with a brass bow chaser and a long gun aimed straight back over the stern, also made of brass. Every sail was raised, every rope was taut, and the first American naval flag flew from a forward mainmast stay, as if fluttering in a strong breeze.

Then Gerritt said, "But I don't think we really need to open the case, do we?"

Jill looked at Robert. "Are you *crazy*? What if there's something hidden inside the boat, or if there's another clue written on that little flag?"

Ben agreed with Jill, and he immediately zipped the wire through the dried pitch.

With the lid up, he could read the tiny lettering on the bows of the ship—it was the USS *Stalwart*, the ship Captain Oakes had commanded when he defeated the British ship in Edgeport Harbor, HMS *Safeguard*—and it was the *Safeguard*'s bell that was hanging on the wall in the school office!

Jill had her headlamp in her hand again, and getting down close, she looked into every opening, checked both sides of every sail—even checked the little deck above the captain's cabin to see if it lifted off.

Ben had looked at a lot of model ships, and this was the best one he'd ever seen, especially the rigging. Every knot was perfect—even the wooden pulleys were carved just right, and each tiny belaying pin locked a rope in its proper place.

After a minute or two Jill straightened up. "I don't see anything."

"Except an amazing model ship, you mean," Ben added.

"Yeah," Gerritt said, "I agree that it's definitely cool—but is *that* gonna save the school? I don't think so."

Ben could feel Robert's impatience.

"All right," he said, "ready for the last one?"

Robert nodded. "Yeah, and let's have a big drumroll for item number three!"

And as Ben pulled the cloth covering off, Gerritt moved in closer with the camera and fluttered his tongue to make a fakey drum sound: "Ba-dur-rum, ba-dur-rum, ba-dur-rummm . . ."

And then he stopped.

Ben stood still, staring, and so did Jill, her eyes popped wide.

It was another display case, but this one had glass on all four sides as well as the top. There was a brass plaque on the wide front, fastened to the wood below the glass panel.

But no one read the plaque—no one needed to.

Because right there, dressed in his Revolutionary War naval uniform, lay the body of Captain Duncan Oakes.

CHAPTER 25

American
Mummy

"Shocked" was not a strong enough word.

Neither was "stunned" or "amazed"—not even "thunderstruck."

Ben could *not* get his mind around this!

He'd been climbing all over the captain's gravestone ever since he was four years old—*outside*, out on the playground of the school! Because *that* was where Captain Oakes was buried—everyone in the whole town knew that! Everyone in the entire *state* knew it—that Duncan Oakes was this weird old guy who had built a school and then had himself buried on the playground—outside!

Except . . . it wasn't true.

Because the man was lying right there, on full display—every ghastly bit of him.

No, that wasn't true either. Because his face was hidden.

Someone had carefully placed a square of blue silk, a covering that went from the top of his forehead down to the high collar of his shirt.

But Ben still saw a glimpse of dark, leathery skin—part of his neck.

And even though the captain was wearing fancy dress gloves, the hands looked thin and bony—the same hands that looked so strong and sure in that painting downstairs.

A shiver ran through him, and Ben thought, It's an American mummy!

Jill whispered, "Shut off the camera, Robert."

"But I want to get a shot of—"

"Turn it *off—now*!"

"All right . . . sorry. It's off," he said.

Ben peeked at Jill—she looked awful . . . pale and tired, and now sort of scared, too.

He felt like he wanted to go put an arm across her shoulders.

And he also felt like he wanted her to come do the same thing for him.

But he needed to be strong now, he had to be Captain Pratt . . . right?

Right.

Speaking softly, he said, "So . . . remember what it said on that engraved message that told all the clues, the message that ended with the oath of secrecy? It said to look for the final safeguard 'only if you must,' because once that last one was found, 'our school will change forever.' I don't know about you guys, but that's *exactly* what just happened for me."

"Yeah, me too," Robert said, "but . . . I think this is really going to do it—save the school, I mean."

Jill stared at him. "I don't get that—how?"

Ben had never seen Gerritt look so uncomfortable. It seemed like he was having to force himself to speak each word, one after the other.

"Well," Robert began, "I know this is gonna sound weird and everything, but when I was in fourth grade? That was when I first sort of started to understand what had really happened to my mom and dad. And I used to stop at their graves over in the churchyard on the way home from school—like, at least two or three times a week, all year long. And I thought about them being down there, with all those other people lying all around them. And . . . well, there's a big backyard at Gram's house, and an apple tree that blossoms every spring. And I thought it might be nice if . . . if they were buried right there, close to home."

He stopped, and Ben could tell it took an effort to make himself continue.

"Anyway, I talked to Gram about it one day, and she said it was a nice idea, but that there were strict laws about where bodies could be buried. And once they *were* buried, there were even stricter laws about moving them." He paused again, smiled sheepishly, and said, "Well, you know me, so I went and studied up on all the Massachusetts laws about burials and graveyards and tombstones and crypts and monuments—I kind of got obsessed. All the laws are online, and there are *tons* of them, and they aren't that hard to understand—they try to use really clear language. And Gram was right—once a body is laid to rest, it's supposed to be left alone. And if there's a gravestone or a monument, it's illegal to mess with that, too."

"Oh!" Jill said. "You're saying that even though this is a school, because the captain is lying dead right *there*, this whole big building is kind of like a giant gravestone!"

Robert nodded. "Right. I mean, we should check it out with the lawyer, but yeah, that's what I think."

Ben said, "Call him—call the lawyer!"

Gerritt made a face. "Now? It's three thirty in the morning."

"So?" said Ben. "The Oakes trust is paying him a *lot* of money—call him! And put it on speaker."

Harold Chamden picked up on the first ring.

"Robert—are you okay? You're not at the police station—listen, don't make *any* statements, not a word to *anybody*, okay? Not a word!"

"We're fine, Mr. Chamden, we're all fine. We're here at the school, up in the cupola on the top of the roof. Sorry to wake you up, but—"

"Wake me up?" The lawyer laughed. "Are you kidding? I've been talking with your grandmother and Jill's and Ben's parents all night—trust me, *nobody* is sleeping!"

Ben said, "You're on speakerphone, Mr.

Chamden—could you talk a little softer? And Robert needs to tell you something."

As Robert began explaining, Ben got out his phone and snapped a photo of the body in the glass coffin and a second shot of the brass plaque on the front of it.

Talking very fast now, Robert said, "So, up here in the cupola? We found Captain Oakes, um, I mean, his body. This is where he's *buried*, except it's more like a mummy, because his body's lying in a glass case, right here. And I was just telling Jill and Ben how I'm pretty sure this means that nobody can do anything to the school, because—"

"Wait, wait . . . ," said the lawyer, "you said his *body* is right there? In plain view?"

Ben spoke up. "Mr. Chamden, this is Ben again, and I just sent you two pictures in a text."

Captain Duncan Oakes
1735 - 1792

They heard the lawyer's phone ding, then heard him tapping, then, "Whoa! That is *incredible*! Hang on a sec . . ."

Ben heard his fingers tapping a keyboard, and then Mr. Chamden began to narrate what he was doing.

"Okay . . . I'm at the website for the Massachusetts General Laws . . . burial, cremation, burial at sea—here we go! Chapter one hundred fourteen, cemeteries and burials. And . . . here it is, section eighteen. Listen to this: 'Any town having within its limits an abandoned or neglected burying ground may take charge of the same and keep it in good order, and may appropriate money therefore, but no property rights shall be violated and no body shall be disinterred. No fence, tomb, monument, or other structure shall be removed or destroyed, but the same may be repaired or restored.' So that's it! It's against the law to even *touch* that body, and no part of the structure around it can be removed or destroyed! Case closed—almost. You need to send me more pictures right away, as many as you have, and then get out of there without alerting the janitors. I'll get the rest of our legal team on this right away, like in the next ten minutes, and

we'll be at the courthouse in Salem at eight thirty—
which is . . . that's less than six hours from now!
And you kids need to get home to bed!"

"Yes, they certainly do!"

The deep voice echoed in the small room, and
the short hairs on the back of Ben's neck stood
up. He stared at the dead man in the glass coffin—
and then spun around.

Lyman!

Lyman was standing behind them on the
ladder, with just his head and shoulders above the
top of the open hatchway—and he had a clear
view of the whole room!

The lawyer said, "Who . . . whose voice was
that?"

Ben gulped, then spoke clearly. "Mr. Chamden,
please turn on a recorder. . . . Is it on?"

After a pause and a click, the lawyer said, "Yes,
I'm recording now."

Ben said, "That was the voice of Jerroald
Lyman, an employee of the Glennley Group. And
he's also been working as a janitor here at the
Oakes School. And he is here in the room with
us." Ben snapped a photo of Lyman and texted it.
"I've just sent you a picture of him."

The lawyer took over. "Mr. Lyman, I am Harold Chamden, and I am an attorney and an officer of the court in Essex County. I represent the three students there with you, and also their parents and guardians. These students have just sent me photographic evidence of what you see there, and I also have evidence that you are right now within the burial monument of Captain Duncan Oakes. The room you see there is defined by law as an ancient burial site. I am now giving you a direct and clear warning that if you make any attempt to disturb that site or any of the artifacts there, or anywhere else in the entire building, such actions will make you *personally* liable for fines and imprisonment under the general laws of the Commonwealth of Massachusetts. Under the law, this discovery of human remains must be reported immediately to the local police, which will be my next phone call, and a uniformed officer will be there inside the next fifteen minutes, possibly sooner. You will need to give the police your full cooperation. The people who will be viewing this gravesite in the next days and weeks will be other state and local police officers, the state medical examiner, and the state archaeologist. Do you understand what I've just told you?"

Lyman answered immediately, and Ben was puzzled by how sincerely and freely he spoke.

"Yes, Mr. Chamden, I understand completely, and I want to assure you that neither I nor the company I work for wants to break any law of any kind, or to be involved in any illegal activity. However, I am *very* concerned to find three young people here inside a town building at three fifteen in the morning, because I also work for the Edgeport Unified School District, and this is a very unusual circumstance."

"Thank you for your concern," said Mr. Chamden. "And as a school employee, you are now legally and personally responsible for escorting students safely downstairs, and you will find their parents and relatives waiting in the school parking lot on the south side of the building, and they will take all the children to their homes. Do you understand your legal responsibility to do this?"

"I do, sir," said Lyman, "and you have my word that I shall do just as you have directed."

Again, Ben could not figure out what was going on, what kind of game the janitor was playing.

The lawyer said, "Ben, I want you to keep

this line open, and if we should get disconnected, call me back immediately. And I'll be there soon, about the time you meet up with your parents. And if there is any problem whatsoever, any one of you can dial 9-1-1. Do you understand?"

Ben said, "Yes. Thanks, Mr. Chamden."

Lyman looked around the room. "Very impressive, and I congratulate you on finding this. *Very* impressive. Well, we'd better get downstairs."

He took a step backward down the ladder.

Ben didn't move, and neither did Jill or Robert.

Ben looked Lyman in the eye. "What're you doing? What kind of trick is this?"

Lyman looked back at him. "There's no trick," he said mildly. "It's very simple—you've won. With all the theme parks and other development projects that the Glennley Group has launched over the past fifteen years, do you think this is the first time we've bumped into graveyards or tombs or ancient burial grounds? They're most often Native American sites, but we are well aware of these kinds of laws. And as I told Mr. Chamden, we don't want to break any laws. Also, I personally believe that it's morally wrong to disturb anyone's final resting place—that's just how I feel, and I don't like it even if a court approves. And now . . ."

The lawyer spoke up through the speaker-phone. "I'm still recording all this. . . ."

Ben was still glaring at Lyman. "You 'don't want to break any laws'—are you kidding? What about when you tried to flood out the whole school last weekend?"

Lyman's face darkened, and he snapped, "There were other—"

He stopped himself, and began again, more quietly. "That was an unfortunate incident, a plumbing failure in an old building. But getting back to what the lawyer was saying, he's right about how everything has changed here, and that is the report I'll make to the people at my company as soon as we're outside. I've had a particular role to play here during this project . . . but now that this has become a legal and moral matter, *my* work is done."

Jill said, "But what about when you stole that whole Underground Railroad station from us? That wasn't exactly *legal*!"

Lyman's eyes flashed a little at that, but he kept his voice calm. "On the contrary. It was my dog, a Rottweiler named Moose, who discovered that hideout after he somehow got trapped inside the north stairwell. There was no indication that anyone else had been inside the school that night—legally or *il*legally—since this is a discussion of what is or has been *lawful*. And once that historically important room was found, my company and I acted quickly and responsibly to preserve it."

Listening, Ben had to agree with Lyman—technically, he probably hadn't broken any laws. And studying the man's eyes, Ben didn't see any anger there now, didn't see any hidden craftiness in his face—if anything, the guy seemed sort of relieved.

Jill wasn't done. "What about Wally? Is he good with all this now?"

Lyman tapped the walkie-talkie clipped to his collar. "Wally, did you hear all of this? You agree that we've finished our work here now, right?"

The speaker sputtered, but it was definitely Wally's voice, and it sounded like a "yes." Lyman clicked the walkie-talkie off, and again he said, "So, we should get downstairs."

It was very odd, but Ben believed Lyman—completely. It was like they were talking with a different person. But he still kept his guard up.

They reached the third-floor hallway, and

as they started down the south stairwell, Robert asked, "So, how did you find us up there?"

"Well," Lyman said, "I had an alarm set for three a.m., because I recalled that some of you had come into the school before at about that time—which is, of course, the best time for covert nighttime action. So, Wally and I made a sweep through all the halls. First off, all the paintings and maps had been covered with that white plastic in the afternoon, and when we got up here, the plastic over that big painting was gone. Then it was just a matter of listening, and we heard faint voices and some other sounds. A strong flashlight on the big painting revealed that hole in the canvas, right at the keyhole—which was brilliant. And using a good stiff piece of wire and a pair of locking pliers, Wally was able to fashion a key that worked in the lock. Once it was open, I climbed up, and he listened in. I was halfway up the steps when I heard you start talking about the . . . corpse."

As they came out of the stairwell into the first-floor hallway, Jill and Robert were both talking at once, telling how shocked they'd been to see that dead body.

239

Ben didn't know whether to smile or frown. Gerritt and Jill had apparently also decided that Lyman wasn't the enemy anymore. It was like they were pals now—old veterans, swapping war stories.

He heard something, and thought it might have been his dad beeping the car horn. "Shh . . . ," he said, "quiet a second. Did you hear that?"

All four of them stood still, and now the sound was very clear.

And loud. And close.

But Ben didn't need to ask what it was, because now he knew.

It was the unmistakable rumble of a diesel engine—a *big* one!

CHAPTER 26

The Beast

Ben whipped around and glared at Lyman, almost spitting in his face.

"You *snake*! All your nicey-nice talk about giving up, and all that friendly chat about the law—all so *Wally* could have time to get outside and fire up the destroyer!"

Lyman shook his head, his eyes wild. "I never—"

But Ben turned away, grabbed Jill's hand, and took off running.

"C'mon, Gerritt!" he shouted. "The front door!"

They blasted outside, and when they rounded the south corner of the school, all three of them stopped short—frozen in place.

Ben shivered, and he squeezed Jill's hand so hard that she said, "Ow!"

He let her hand go, then instantly wished he hadn't. The view before them was like a scene from a horror movie.

In the orange glow of the streetlights, he saw that the huge tractor treads of the demolition excavator had chewed up the pavement on Washington Street, broken the granite curb stones, and now they were grinding a path across the south lawn, straight toward the school. Three maple trees, each thirty or forty feet tall, had already been knocked down, brushed aside like weeds by the massive machine.

As Ben watched, almost hypnotized, the enormous hydraulic arm began to unfold, rising up and reaching forward, its yellow-and-black tendons lit by the lamps along the harbor walk. The clanking treads and the whine and roar of the big engine made it hard to think.

Something rushed past him, and Ben was startled—then he realized it was Lyman, running toward the machine, which surprised him even more.

"You guys get over there!" Ben shouted to Jill

and Robert, pointing toward the water, and he took off after Lyman.

The man had such long legs that he got to the tractor a good fifteen seconds before Ben, and he'd run around to the far side, where the cab was. Ben followed, then stopped as close as he dared—the noise was deafening.

Inside the cab, Wally was hunched over the controls, his hands quickly moving from lever to lever as he guided the machine across the lawn. The long arm, now up at least sixty feet above them, was poised like a giant cobra. Another twenty feet of forward travel, and the south corner of the school would be in striking range.

Lyman cupped his hands around his mouth. *"Wally!"*

He screamed the name a second time, even louder. *"WALLY!"*

But if Wally heard him, he gave no sign of it. The light from the control gauges cast a dim greenish glow up onto his face, and Ben thought the guy looked totally out of it. Glancing to his left, Ben saw that Jill and Gerritt hadn't gone to the harbor walk— they'd followed him. Ben was about to yell something to Jill when Lyman did an astonishing thing.

With a running leap, he landed with both feet on the moving treads, then quickly stepped onto the deck beside the door of the cab. He pounded on the glass with a fist, and Wally jumped as if he'd been stuck with a pin, completely surprised.

He didn't open the door and he didn't slow down.

But he did slide back the window on the door, and when Lyman pointed at his ears, the sound of the engine backed down.

Ben could hear them shouting.

"You can't do this, Wally! Really, you can't!"

"I *heard* you," Wally bellowed. "You surrendered to those stinking kids! You said, 'You've won'! You're a *traitor*!"

Lyman shook his head, his long face earnest and serious.

"I'm not a traitor, Wally. I had a *job* here, that's all. And that gravesite? It changes everything. There's a dead *human being* up there. If no one had found it until after the building came down, that wouldn't have been our fault. But it's *there*, and we *know* it's there. And now it's wrong to even touch the place. The law wins, Wally. You should know that by now—the law *always* wins!"

"Oh yeah?" screamed Wally. "Let's see how the law deals with *this*!"

He jammed the window shut and faced forward again. Lyman kept pounding on the glass, but Wally ignored him. The exhaust pipe blasted dense smoke and sparks into the night air, and the tractor surged forward, faster than before. Wally flipped a switch, and two powerful headlights on the front of the cab lit up the whole south side of the school.

Lyman got his fingers into the crack of the control cab door and began to pull, but Wally suddenly shoved the door open wide and knocked him backward. Lyman stumbled onto the clanking treads and fell to his side, hitting his head before tumbling the four feet to the ground. He lay still.

Jill reached him first. "Mr. Lyman! Mr. Lyman!"

There was a cut on the side of his head, but he opened his eyes and smiled weakly at Jill. And when he saw Ben and Robert, he croaked, "Hurry, call the police!"

But Mr. Chamden already had.

A cruiser pulled into the bus turnaround, lights flashing and siren pulsing. Ben ran toward it, waving his arms, and then the car jumped the curb and sped across the lawn, coming to a stop fifteen feet in front of the advancing excavator.

Both officers jumped out, leaving the doors open wide. They stood side by side, each taking the same stance: one hand held out in front, palm open, and the other hand at the hip, close to their service weapons.

The message was clear, and Wally got it.

The machine stopped moving forward, the diesel engine slowed to a quiet purr, then clattered to a complete stop. In the sudden silence, Ben could hear waves, lapping against the seawall.

The officers walked to the side of the machine, and when Wally opened the cab door and climbed awkwardly to the ground, one of them put handcuffs on him, while the other one read him his rights. They started to lead him toward the cruiser, but Wally said something, and the men nodded and brought him over to Lyman, who was now sitting up on the grass.

"You okay, Jerry? I'm . . . I'm sorry you got hurt."

"I know, Wally. I'll be fine. And I'll come see you later this morning, I promise."

Ben watched Wally walk away toward the police car. Then he looked at Lyman.

He squatted down so he could look him in the eye, and said, "Mr. Lyman? I want to apologize too—for accusing you of helping Wally try to do that."

Lyman nodded. "I understand. But it's like I was telling Wally—I really was just doing a job here. I actually admire you, and your friends, too. It's been an honor." He paused and gave Ben a crooked smile. "And, if you promise not to tell my boss, I'll let you in on a big secret. I am *very* happy that it's turned out this way—no kidding!"

Lyman held out a hand. Ben shook it, and as he smiled into the man's face, he'd never felt more grown-up in his life.

As he stood up, he heard someone call his name. He turned to his left and saw his dad and mom running across the lawn, both of them looking scared.

He waved, and when his mom yelled, "Are you all right?" he called back, "Yeah, I'm fine."

As Ben watched them, he couldn't stop smiling. It wasn't just because he was glad to see them, or because it was good to feel so loved.

He smiled because, as they hurried toward him, they were holding hands.

CHAPTER 27

Historic

"You have to sit over on *that* side—you're ruining the trim!"

Jill made a face. "I don't care about the trim. I'm sitting on *this* side of the boat because I want to sit next to *you*. End of discussion."

Ben laughed, and then said, "Fine. But don't blame me if you never learn how to sail."

"Who said I wanted to learn how to sail?"

School had been over for two weeks, and the media storm whipped up by their discoveries had mostly died down. A news crew from somewhere like Moscow or Rio de Janeiro would still show up in town every few days, but it was nothing like that first week. The interviews had been nonstop, at least three a day. The whole account of the discoveries had already been featured in magazines and newspapers all around the world—not to mention the Internet explosion. Ben thought the best story he'd seen was the one in the Sunday *Boston Globe*, a huge feature with a lot of good photos. The last time he'd checked, there were thirty-three YouTube videos about the Oakes School, and the one Gerritt had made had already pulled in more than six million hits.

But the world was moving on to other news.

He'd been glad to learn that all the charges against Wally had been dropped, and Jill and Robert were glad about that too. The guy had just taken everything too personally.

Something Jill had to keep warning me about. . . .

And even there at the end, he'd thought the worst about Lyman. Not taking things personally? That was a tough one.

As part of Wally's deal, the Glennley Group had agreed to pay for all the repairs to the street and the school grounds—three new maple trees had already been replanted.

No one had seen Lyman since that morning, sitting on the lawn outside the school with a gash on the side of his head. Ben hoped that he was keeping his promise about taking Wally for a long cruise.

Ben pulled on the sheet to try to pick up some speed and make the boat flatten out, get it to plane better. It was hopeless . . . unless he could make Jill move to the other side of the boat. He smiled to himself and paid out the sheet again.

The Glennley Group had issued a statement about their decision to work with the town to untangle the financial problems caused by the sudden cancellation of the Tall Ships Ahoy! project. It was a huge mess.

The Captain Oakes trust was taking an active role in that process. The trustees had unanimously decided that in order to help with "the welfare, preservation, and continuing operation of the Captain Duncan Oakes School," the trust should make a large, anonymous donation to the town— so that the taxpayers of Edgeport would not have to bear any extra burdens, and so that the Glennley Group could be fully repaid and sent packing as quickly as possible. Mr. Rydens wasn't worried about the expenses. "As long as we still have five or ten million left to keep investing, the trust will be fine. And who knows, in another century or two, someone else may want to try to take that land and use it to build a spaceport or something. But we shall be ready for them. When it comes to growing money, there is nothing quite like *time*."

It was a relief to be out on the water. He and Jill and Robert and the other Keepers had become local celebrities—which was surprisingly annoying. And tiring.

But Ben tried to push all that out of his mind, and just sail.

Even sailing had changed for him, especially racing.

He had won the first official race of the season, and Gerritt had won the next, even-steven. It was still just as fun, but winning didn't seem to matter quite as much as it used to. Even Gerritt was a little more relaxed about racing. There was still plenty of trash talk, but that was different too.

Everything was different.

"It was nice, what you did for Robert. He's going to love taking a trip on your dad's boat. And he's going to end up being your best friend, you know."

Ben looked sideways at her. "I thought you were going to be my best friend."

She smiled, but didn't answer. There wasn't any need to.

"Ready about!" he said, but it was a casual command.

He eased the boat around, and they both shifted to the other side. There wasn't much of a breeze—just enough to make decent headway. With horrible trim.

"Yeah," he said, "I thought about asking you to come. Really, that was my first idea. But I knew you weren't exactly crazy about sailing."

Jill wrinkled her nose. "No offense, but the idea of being stuck on a boat like the *Tempus Fugit* for three weeks? That would drive me crazy—even if I was with someone I liked—even someone I *really* liked." She paused. "No, I meant what I said. Asking Robert to go along was a nice thing, and he's going to have a great time."

It was July now, and the hours they'd spent on his boat and on the beach had been good for both of them. But better for Jill, he decided. She looked just right. The paleness of the long school year was gone from her face. It was a face he never got tired of looking at.

The school was never going to be the same, just like Captain Oakes had warned. On this tack, he had a clear view of the place, there on the shore, dominating the skyline—exactly where it belonged.

Jill was staring in the same direction.

"So . . . ," he said, "what do you see when you look at the school now?"

"I see you and Robert and Mr. Keane and Tom Benton and Lyman and Wally and Mrs. Sinclair and Mrs. Hinman . . . and Captain Oakes . . . and a million other people, and all that stuff we found." She paused a moment, and gave him a half smile. "But mostly, I see you."

Ben smiled back. "I'm good with that."

He didn't want to spoil things by telling her what he saw.

Because his view was a lot more analytical. When he looked at the school now, he saw the past and the present and the future, all jumbled up together. Captain Oakes had reached out from his grave and pressed a gold coin into his hand. And from now on, Ben knew that *he* was an important part of the history of this place—all the Keepers were.

Changes? Yes. But as far as he could tell, the changes were going to be good.

The plan that the school board had proposed was pretty simple. The brand-new middle school on the other side of town was going to become the junior high school. And thanks to another large, anonymous cash donation, there were going to be significant improvements made to the Oakes School.

The Historical Society was involved, too. If those improvements could be made quickly enough, then starting next summer, the school would be open during July and August as a museum—sort of like the House of the Seven Gables and Nathaniel Hawthorne's house in Salem. There would be weekly visiting hours so people could come and see the legacy of Captain Duncan Oakes—including his very own dead body.

Ben had thought about *that* quite a bit. And he and Robert had talked about it too—they'd had two sleepovers since school let out.

Because that *thing* in the coffin—that wasn't the person. He was sure of that. And he was pretty sure Captain Oakes had known that too.

But it still amazed him to think how Captain Oakes had used all his skills, all his resources, everything he had—including his very own body— to protect something that he felt sure was worth protecting.

Big ideas.

Ben was tired of big ideas.

He wanted to think about smaller ideas for a while. The big ones weren't going to go anywhere.

Jill was leaning toward him, with one hand over the side, fingertips trailing in the water. She sat that way every time they went out. It made the boat tilt even worse, but Ben didn't care.

"And your mom and dad?" she asked. "Are things better?"

"Yeah," he said, "they seem pretty good. Still not back together, not in the same house yet. But this trip? Being stuck on a boat for three weeks is gonna be just right for them. I've got a good feeling about it."

Ben took another quick sideways look at her, then turned the other way and smiled. He had a good feeling about Jill, too. They hadn't kissed yet, but he was pretty sure it was going to happen.

And he was pretty sure that she was pretty sure about it too.

That would be historic.

But there was no big rush. The summer was just beginning.

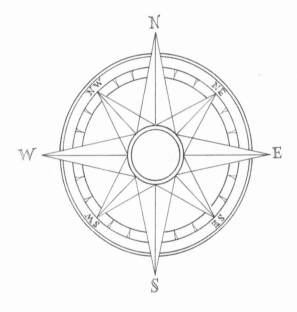

Books by Andrew Clements

Benjamin Pratt & the Keepers of the School
#1: We the Children
#2: Fear Itself
#3: The Whites of Their Eyes
#4: In Harm's Way
#5: We Hold These Truths
•
Big Al
Big Al and Shrimpy
Dogku
The Handiest Things in the World
A Million Dots
•
About Average
Extra Credit
Frindle
The Jacket
Jake Drake, Bully Buster
Jake Drake, Class Clown
Jake Drake, Know-It-All
Jake Drake, Teacher's Pet
The Janitor's Boy
The Landry News
The Last Holiday Concert
Lost and Found
Lunch Money
The Map Trap
No Talking
The Report Card
Room One
The School Story
Troublemaker
A Week in the Woods

CHECK OUT ANDREW CLEMENTS'S
NEWEST BOOK
THE MAP TRAP

When the fire alarm began to beep and blink on Tuesday morning, the first thing Miss Wheeling thought about was her hair. She'd been outside on bus duty forty minutes ago, and it was a bright October day, moist and windy—the worst kind of weather for her hair. Couldn't the principal have put off this drill for a couple of days?

It was free-activity time near the end of homeroom, and she clapped her hands sharply. "All right, everyone, this is a fire drill. Line up quickly, and I want you *quiet*! And don't clean up, don't do anything except get in line right *now*!"

She wrestled a scarf around her hair, and then, clutching her clipboard, Miss Wheeling led her homeroom students down the hall, past the gym, and straight outside toward their assigned spot along the playground fence. She noted with pride that hers was one of the first groups out of the building—pretty good for a brand-new teacher! She hoped the principal would notice.

She tried to remember the last time she'd been part of a fire drill, but she couldn't get a clear picture. . . . It had probably been during high school—about five years ago, back when she was just Holly Wheeling, that girl who was crazy about insects.

She heard some loud whispering behind her, but she didn't need to look to know who it was. This class had a handful of very gabby kids.

"Annie and Kelley? I asked you *not* to talk. A fire drill is serious business."

She still felt amazed every time she realized that now she was Miss Wheeling, *the teacher*. She looked young, she felt young—she *was* young, only twenty-three years old. In fact, her own little brother was twelve, the same age as most of her students. And she was *very* glad that her family lived in Cedar Falls, Iowa, instead of Harper's Grove, Illinois—the town where she now lived and worked. The thought of being Carl's teacher? It was enough to give a girl nightmares.

The wind kicked up a flurry of dead leaves along the playground fence, and Miss Wheeling held the corners of her scarf tightly under her chin. But she knew it was hopeless. This was going to be a bad hair day—mega-bad. She'd been trying to set an appointment for a haircut for the past three weeks, but her first months as a new teacher had been insanely busy. Not that haircuts ever helped much. Her hair was very full, extremely curly, and almost impossible to style. She'd been fighting with it almost every day since she was about six years old. And losing.

All the classes were outside now, and she saw Mrs. Buckley at the far side of the playground. The principal was moving from teacher to teacher, checking off each group.

Miss Wheeling whipped her scarf off her head and stuffed it into the back pocket of her slacks. She looked at her clipboard and called out, "Billy Atkinson?"

"Here."

"Jada Bartlett?"

"Present."

"Carson Burr?"

"Present."

Miss Wheeling hurried through the names as the principal came nearer, and finally called out, "Alton Ziegler?"

Nothing.

She called the name again. "Alton Ziegler?"

The principal was close now, talking with Mr. Troy, the other sixth-grade teacher.

Desperate, Miss Wheeling flipped to her attendance sheets . . . but Alton was definitely present today. She was certain that she'd seen him just half an hour ago, and she was sure—

"Good morning, Miss Wheeling." Mrs. Buckley smiled at her and then at the kids. "Is your class all accounted for?"

"I'm . . . I'm sorry, but Alton Ziegler's not here." Miss Wheeling felt her face growing pale, and her hands were cold and clammy. She felt light-headed.

The principal frowned. "Was he in homeroom when you took attendance?"

"Oh . . . oh, yes! I checked him off, see?" Helplessly, Miss Wheeling held out her clipboard.

Mrs. Buckley didn't look at it. With a sharp edge to her voice, she said, "I'll stay with your class. Go and find him. Right now."

Miss Wheeling half walked, half ran to the gym door, and she could feel the eyes of everyone in the school watching her—and watching the way her hair bounced around as she ran.

Breathless now, she sprinted to her classroom door, but it was locked—and she didn't have a key.

As she started to turn to go find the janitor, she spotted something on the far side of the room, over beyond the desks, by the windows. Something on the floor.

It was a shoe, a boy's sneaker.

Leaning forward, she pressed her nose against the glass and cupped her hands around her eyes and forehead to block the glare from the hallway lights.

It was definitely a shoe—and also an ankle, plus six inches of a leg . . . wearing blue jeans!

With one hand she banged on the door, still looking at that foot. She called out, "Alton? Alton . . . ? Is that you? *Alton!* Answer me!"

The shoe, the foot, the leg—nothing moved.

Miss Wheeling yelled down the hallway. "Mr. Sims? *Mr. Sims!* Can you hear me?"

"I'm in the front hall," he called back. "What's up?"

"An emergency in room forty-three! Bring a key, and *hurry!*"

Miss Wheeling heard a sharp *crack* as a wooden broom handle hit the floor, and then jangling keys as the janitor came around the corner at a dead run. A moment later he unlocked her door and shoved it open.

She dashed in, fearing the worst. Rounding the last row of desks along the windows, Miss Wheeling stopped—and stared.

She had a clear view of the whole scene—shoe, ankle, leg . . . the entire boy. Alton Zeigler was propped up on his elbows in a patch of sunlight. White wires from a small iPod ran to his ears, and a large sheet of paper lay before him, with markers and colored pencils spread about. He held a red pen in his right hand, and he was humming a tune she didn't know. Mr. Sims stood beside her.

Miss Wheeling reached out her toe and tapped Alton's foot, and he jumped like he'd been stung by a bee. He spun around, then smiled and pulled out his earbuds. He glanced from Miss Wheeling to the janitor.

"Hi—what are you guys doing here?"

Holly Wheeling had trouble finding words—all her fear had turned to anger. She wanted to shout, *What are* we *doing here? What in the world are* you *doing here?!*

But that would have been pointless, because it was perfectly clear what Alton Zeigler was doing here.

He was making a map.